I0450758

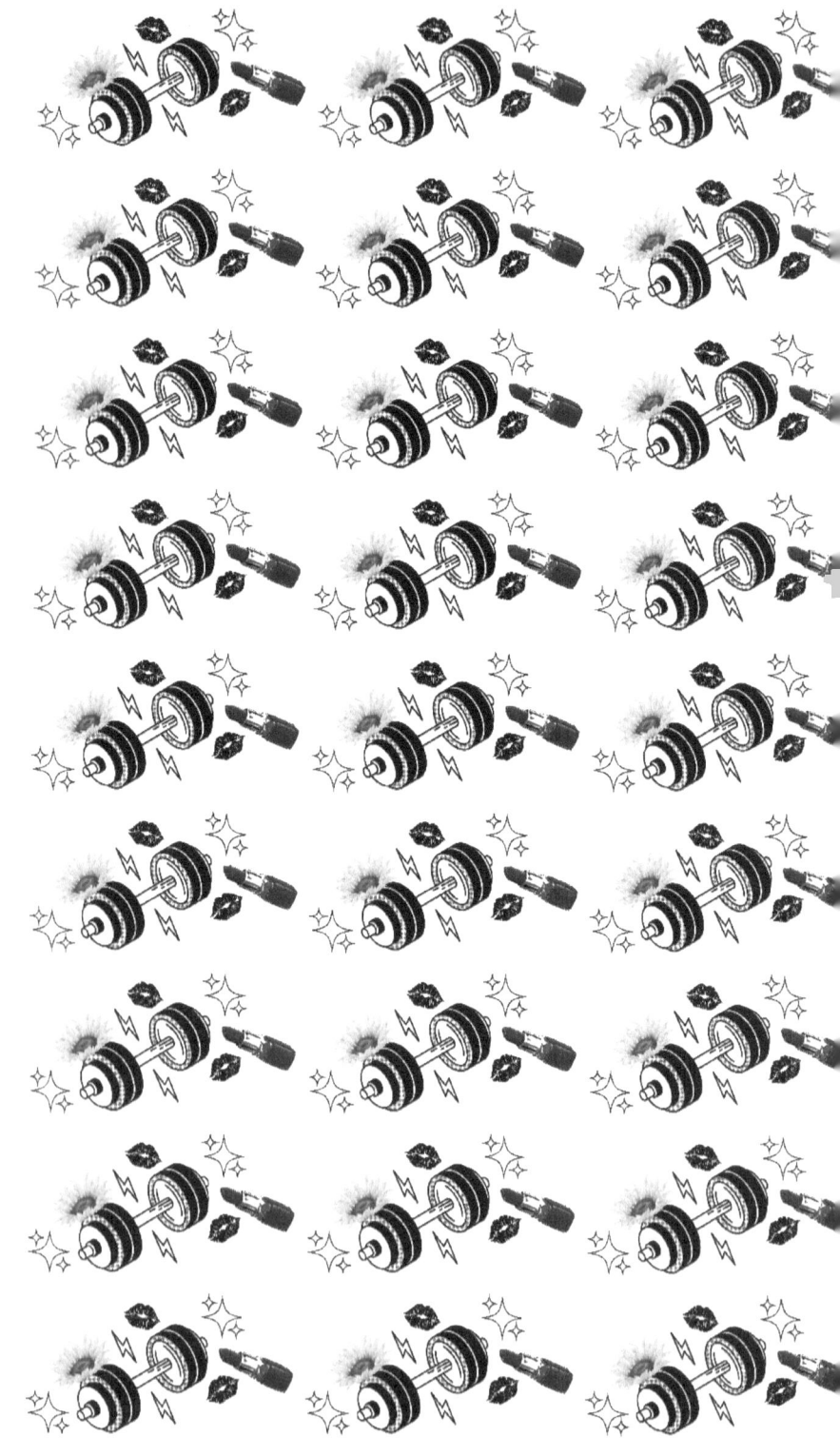

# ROPE
# BREAK

# Rope Break

## J.L. Minyard

CENTURION
BOOKS

This book is a work of fiction. Names, characters, places, and incidents are either products of the author's imagination or are used fictitiously. Any semblance to actual persons, living or dead, events, or locales is entirely coincidental.

**ROPE BREAK © 2025 by Jessica Minyard**

**hello@jessicaminyard.com**

Cover by Cormar Covers

Interior graphics by mgsdesiigns / eBook map by Books and Moods

Editing by Nina Fiegl, Romance Editor s.p.

ISBN: 978-1-957004-17-4

eBook ISBN: 978-1-957004-16-7

20251002

# Content Notes

This book contains material that may be sensitive to some readers. CWs: Explicit sex and language, Dom/sub dynamics, spanking, mild degradation, Shibari, unprotected sex, gun violence (off-page, historical), death of a sibling (off-page, historical), trauma due to gun violence, religion and religious discourse.

As the body without the spirit is dead, so faith without deeds is dead.

(James 2:26)

# INTRODUCTION

Dear Reader,

*Rope Break* is a short kinky romance novella but it is also a small response to the gun violence epidemic in America (because I contain multitudes).

I don't think I will ever have enough words to describe the feeling of raising children in this country. Of sending them to school the day after yet another deadly shooting.

I don't think I have enough words to convey how horrific, how morally bankrupt, I find our government and our politicians, who have decided that the murder of children is an acceptable price to pay to avoid reform and common-sense gun laws. Just so people can keep their assault weapons (when we all know y'all ain't rising up against a tyrannical government anyway).

Columbine should have been enough. Sandy Hook should have been enough. Uvalde should have been enough. How many dead children will be enough? How many devasted families and communities and neighborhoods will be enough? How many school hallways painted with blood do we, as a nation, need to see?

*Rope Break* tackles some heavy topics in not very many words, and I understand it may not be to everyone's tastes. It was my intention to address this subject with sensitivity, nuance, hope, and even a little bit of angsty yearning (it is still a romance, after all).

If my story inspires you to take action, or learn a little more about gun sense, here are some good places to start:

- https://momsdemandaction.org/

- https://studentsdemandaction.org/

- https://everytownsupportfund.org/

- https://www.sandyhookpromise.org/

Take care of yourself and your neighbors,
Jessica

# Chapter One
## Gideon

Mrs. Della was pushing ninety and was firmly convinced her guest bedroom was haunted.

This was the third time Gideon had been out to her house in as many months. The tiny woman—she only came up to his elbow—followed closely behind him as he stopped in the doorway to sprinkle holy water around the frame.

"In the name of the Father, and of the Son, and of the Holy Spirit."

Mrs. Della made the sign of the cross, a wooden rosary wrapped around her wrinkled hands. "Amen."

Gideon moved into the room, flicking the aspergillum as he went. "Lord Jesus Christ, we come before You today to clean this room." Sprinkle, sprinkle. "By Your power, we command all evil spirits to depart this place. We ask that You fill this home with peace and love, and may Your angels guard over Your devoted child, Della Robinson."

Mrs. Della nodded as he spoke, her white hair flopping like dandelion fluffs.

"Let us pray." He held out a hand.

Della took it, holding her rosary to her lips.

"Our Father, who art in heaven, hallowed be thy name; thy kingdom come; thy will be done; on earth as it is in heaven. Give us this day our daily bread; and forgive us our trespasses, as we forgive those who trespass against us; and lead us not into temptation; but deliver us from evil." Gideon closed his eyes and tipped his head back. Mrs. Della seemed to like a little bit of drama with her exorcisms.

Did he really believe there was an evil demonic spirit haunting the pastel pink and blue guest room? No, he didn't. Battling demons was just part of the job description.

"Amen," he intoned, deepening his voice.

"Amen!" Della practically cheered then placed the rosary over her heart. "Oh, thank you, Father. Your visits always balm the soul." She patted his arm like he was a favored grandchild and not a grown man. "Now, come have some tea. I baked my state fair winning lemon bars for you."

Okay, so maybe Mrs. Della was his favorite parishioner, and he would show up to cleanse her house every time she asked, because she *always* baked him lemon bars.

"I wouldn't want to impose."

She waved his concerns away. "Oh, nonsense. You kids are too skinny these days. I like a meaty man. You know my husband—God rest his soul—was a tractor pull champion. Now *that* was a man." She bustled him to the kitchen table.

Gideon was well aware—maybe too aware—about Mr. Robinson's exploits. He'd passed about three years ago, before Gideon transferred to Cedar Creek. The small country church had trouble retaining priests because anyone who was any good got pulled to the bigger parishes.

Gideon had volunteered for the position because he wanted to get away from a large congregation. There was something so impersonal about them—hundreds and hundreds of vague faces in a sea of vague faces. He'd felt invisible even though he was the star of the show. There'd been a strange type of loneliness hollowing him from the inside out, and he thought the transfer would help.

And it had, a little bit. He felt more seen here, in a quiet two-stoplight town, surrounded by parishioners like Della Robinson. He felt that these people knew him, just a little bit, even if they could know nothing about the dark stain on his soul.

Mrs. Della set a plate of lemon bars in front of him on the table. "You know, it's so refreshing to see a man of your age leading our congregation. Maybe it will bring some young people back to church." A sweating glass of sweet tea followed.

He hummed, inhaling the buttery scent permeating the air.

Young people leaving the church may have been a mystery to Della, but Gideon thought it was rather obvious. They didn't need some guy in a fancy robe telling them how to be good humans. They saw through the hypocrisy of the Church, of religious people who preached the Gospel and used Bible quotes to defend their bigotry and hatred.

Gideon wondered if he'd get as many lemon bars if Della was aware of his sexuality, if she knew he spent most of his free time writing articles for liberal news outlets and arguing with hateful keyboard warriors in Facebook comment sections. It was his favorite pastime.

Gideon took a bite, the flavor exploding across his tongue.

Yes, his frequent exorcisms were worth every bite.

After she'd seen him fed, Gideon packed up his effects in a well-worn brown messenger bag, slinging it across his chest as Della waved him away from her wisteria-covered porch.

She'd given him an aluminum tray of lemon bars to take to the diner. Delivering baked goods was not in his job description, but Della lived down one of the little side streets right off West Main, and the diner was only a couple of streets over. It only took him about ten minutes to walk.

He liked walking. He liked exploring the little town he'd found himself in. He'd never imagined that this would be where he found himself after all these years—in the middle of Kentucky, as a priest in a small town that looked like it could adorn the front of a postcard.

But since that one day, when he was seventeen, nothing in his life had gone according to plan. So he really shouldn't be surprised.

The diner wasn't a diner in the traditional sense; it was a salmon-pink house from 1902 that had been renovated and restored several times. It had been bought and sold, and renamed recently, but Gideon learned that it used to be called Creekside Diner and everyone still referred to it as "the diner" or "the Creek", much to the chagrin of the new owners who were trying to rebrand it as Sweetwater Bar and Grill. He'd also heard there had been protest T-shirts and a petition made.

There was a wraparound porch with outdoor seating under hanging twinkle lights; the gardens were meticulously maintained with some kind of fancy bushes and sprays of purple hydrangeas.

Gideon hurried up the white-washed front steps and knocked the door open with his hip, careful not to drop his delivery.

There was an authentic, open-24/7 diner across town, if you went through both of the stop lights, but they didn't get Della's lemon bars.

Creekside opened to an old stone fireplace. To the left, there was a small bar area, sunlight glinting off the wall of Kentucky bourbons—*only* Kentucky bourbons because the Creek was always on-brand. To the right was the main dining area, an airy large open space full of mismatched tables and chairs. The effect was homey and cozy and rustic.

Gideon went left.

"Father," Theo, the man behind the shiny bar, greeted and smiled broadly when he caught sight of the tray Gideon carried.

"Theo." Gideon slid the tray of lemon bars across to him. "I'm under strict instruction to make sure these are evenly distributed this time."

Theo grinned, sniffing at the tray. "It wasn't me last time, I swear. Vinny took, like, five home."

Vinny was the head pastry chef, and Gideon couldn't decide if the man just really loved Della's lemon bars or was trying to reverse engineer them since she wouldn't give up the recipe. Not until she was dead, she said.

Gideon slid onto one of the high-backed chairs, sitting his bag on the chair beside him.

"Something to drink, Father?"

"Bourbon neat, please. Top shelf."

Judging by Theo's raised eyebrows, it may have been a little early for hard liquor, but there was nothing in Gideon's vows that prohibited alcohol. He was Catholic. They did drink wine every Sunday. He was just supposed to remember himself in public, remember that he was an example to other people. One drink was fine. Falling down drunk off his chair would not be.

Theo sat the drink in front of Gideon and went back to his other duties.

Gideon stared at the dark liquid, simultaneously wanting to get lost in its depths and knowing that was impossible. It would be like drowning. And he wouldn't be able to come back from that.

He sucked in a breath, chest suddenly tight, and threw back the bourbon, the alcohol stinging his nostrils and throat bringing him back to his body. To this moment. His duties.

His hot fingers left spectral prints on the glass as he slid it back towards Theo.

An uneasy feeling crawled across the back of his neck, like the brush of fingertips or the prickle of a spider walking across your hand.

He felt watched.

# CHAPTER TWO
## AUSTIN

Austin didn't believe in ghosts, but one just walked into Sweetwater and took a seat at the bar.

The man had caught Austin's attention immediately, not only because he was tall and broad, and had blond curls falling over his forehead. It was early afternoon, and they were some of the only patrons in the restaurant, so Austin had noticed.

Austin liked to drop by the cozy restaurant for lunch because it was close to his tattoo shop; he liked their booze and their chicken salad sandwiches, which were part of the lunch menu only. After he finished his lunch, he'd opened his sketchbook to keep working on the design of a back piece for a client.

He'd been so struck by the man's golden hair and bright smile, against his austere black clothes and strong straight jawline, he'd been compelled to find a new page and start sketching.

Curls, jaw, the line of the man's throat, and his Adam's apple bobbing as he swallowed his shot of bourbon. His sleeves were rolled up to the elbow, exposing tanned skin and the long, lean muscles of his forearms.

He was too pretty for the little white collar at his throat, so stark against the black. The fact that he was so clearly off limits made him even more interesting.

Austin didn't realize quite how hard he was staring until the man turned his head and immediately caught his gaze.

That was when Austin saw the ghost.

The man had a pair of brilliant blue eyes—bluer than the sky, bluer than the ocean. So blue they were sharp like glass.

Austin's breath caught in his throat. He knew those eyes … or he had known them, a long time ago.

The man's hair was longer now; he'd kept the curls short when they were in high school. His brow furrowed as if the phenomenon of recognition had caught him too.

Austin imagined he also looked vastly different from the scrawny, acne-ridden teen he'd been the last time they'd seen each other.

When was that? His brother's funeral, maybe? Because then, the man had run.

Gideon Gray had run. His dead older brother's best friend had run.

Austin could barely remember his brother's funeral. The day was a blur of tears, his mother's quiet sobbing, condolences from distant family members he'd never met before, and the sticky, sweet smell of flowers people had sent. Austin couldn't handle flowers of any kind since that day.

They all smelled like death. They all brought him back to that broken, hollow thirteen-year-old boy who had just lost his hero.

He remembered Gideon, though, who was practically family, since he and Luke had been inseparable.

Gideon had looked the way Austin felt: empty. His bright eyes were dull, lifeless, and rimmed red, his cheeks carved out and gaunt. He hadn't made any noise, no mawkish displays over the altar or next to Luke's urn. Just silence. That day and all the days after.

It had pissed Austin off then; of all the people who should have been there, who knew what he was feeling and going through, it should have been Gideon.

But then life happened, as it so often did, and those feelings dulled like the edge of a used knife. That knife stuck in his ribs now, though, painful and sharp, stealing his breath.

Did Gideon feel the same way?

He might, judging by the way he swallowed and his mouth gaped, like his world had suddenly stopped turning too.

Austin dropped his eyes to his sketchbook, where Gideon's face looked back up at him, somehow so familiar and so different rendered in ink.

A shadow fell over the creamy pages.

Austin looked up.

Gideon stood next to Austin's table, his hand on the back of the seat across from Austin. He wasn't running this time.

Austin flipped the sketchbook closed, trapping his pen and napkin between the pages. Hopefully, he'd been quick enough.

"May I?" Gideon gestured toward the empty seat he held.

Austin found his throat dry, so he just nodded. He was woefully underprepared for whatever conversation they were about to have.

Gideon sat, carefully arranging his long limbs. He crossed his legs; his black slacks ended in a pair of all-black high-top Nikes. One hand landed on his knee and the other casually on the table, tendons flexing under his skin.

Sun from the front windows reflected off his golden head, almost creating a halo, which was terribly ironic.

Gideon Gray had always been one of the cool kids. Luke too. They were at the top of the social food chain. Rebels, but didn't really get into serious trouble and still got good grades. When Luke wanted to play baseball, Gideon followed and turned out to be some kind of baseball prodigy.

Austin would go to games to support his brother when, in reality, it was to watch Gideon run bases in his tight uniform.

Not that he ever noticed. They were seniors, and Austin was just a freshman.

To be fair, he'd worshipped them both, for very different reasons.

Austin knew Gideon was gay. It wasn't really a secret, but he also wasn't really out when they were teenagers. They went to a large public high school in a blue-dot city, so there were other out queer kids, but Gideon never dated.

For a while, Austin thought there may have been something between his brother and Gideon. He finally got brave enough to ask. Luke had laughed, ruffled his hair, and said Gideon was hot as fuck but Luke was unfortunately straight.

Gideon's mouth tipped up now, and heat wormed through Austin's chest.

"I almost didn't recognize you," Gideon said.

"Yeah, you either." Austin's gaze wandered to the white collar at his throat. "Catholicism. Really, Gray?"

Gideon's slight smile disappeared, and his gaze flicked off into the distance. "I don't think this is the best place to have this conversation."

Austin slouched obstinately in his chair. "Why not? There's no one else here."

At this hour, the place was practically deserted, except for a few other regulars and the bartender.

"There's a lot ... I have a lot to explain. A lot to say." His piercing blue eyes found Austin again, pinioning him to his chair. "Come to St. Benedict's tonight. Please." The tone of his voice changed on the last word. It was a plea, dragged from his throat.

It was compelling to hear a man like Gideon Gray beg. The heat in Austin's chest morphed—a strange mix of anger and desire he knew was forbidden, which just made it that much worse.

But Austin knew he'd be showing up at Gideon's church later.

# CHAPTER THREE

## GIDEON

Gideon was falling apart.

He had been trying to hold the shattered, jagged pieces of himself together for years now. His collar, his vows, and his devotion to the church were all supposed to fix him. The church was supposed to be his salvation, his sanctuary. This small town, the same.

And now they were both ruined.

He supposed it was only a matter of time before his past caught up to him. It always did, in some way, shape, or form.

A memory. A sound. A smell.

He hadn't expected his reckoning to come in the shape of a person.

Luke's little brother was barely recognizable. His brown hair was long on top, streaked with blond. Gideon couldn't tell if it was natural or not. Every inch of Austin's exposed skin was covered with tattoos, the ink thick around his throat. There were long-stemmed roses above each dark eyebrow. He had been gangly as a teenager but had grown into his limbs, and the lines of his body were lean.

As soon as they made eye contact in the Creek, Gideon's heart stopped. His breath had come short. Because he knew he hadn't done right by Austin and had been running from that mistake, and so many others, for most of his adult life.

He had abandoned a scared, devastated boy who, if Gideon could judge by Austin's scowl and body language, was an angry young man. He had every right to be angry. Gideon could handle his anger. He had been bracing himself to handle as much for so many years.

What he shouldn't have done was invite Austin to St. Benedict's. St. Benedict's was his home, his sanctuary, and his safety.

It was late. He almost hoped Austin had changed his mind and wouldn't show.

Gideon was lighting the altar candles with a long wooden match, the yellow flames flickering against the red glass of their sconces, when the doors to the vestibule opened and closed.

He heard Austin's footfalls as he came up the steps of the narthex and walked down the center aisle of the sanctuary.

"Do churches normally stay open this late?" Austin's voice echoed in the empty building. "Or am I just an exception?"

Gideon's hands were shaking.

He did usually try to leave the building open each night for as long as possible, for anyone who needed safety or shelter or food. There was a large parishioner-led food pantry in the vestibule. He was bound and determined to turn the church into a place where people found comfort when they needed it most.

"Why are you here?" he finally said.

"You asked me to come."

Gideon huffed, some of the tension bleeding from his shoulders. "No, why are you here, in this town specifically?"

He still hadn't looked at Austin, but he heard the rustling of clothes, like Austin had shoved his hands in his pockets.

"Rent's cheap. My small business loan went farther."

Now Gideon was surprised. He took a step back so he could angle his body towards Austin.

He indeed had his hands in the pockets of his tight jeans, and was practically glaring at the altar and the sanctuary.

A disappointed frown curved his mouth down like he was personally offended by the candles and the statuary.

"What business?"

"Sabbath Ink. It's my shop."

Gideon knew the place. It was on the edge of town, right off the highway that would take you to the nearest big city.

"I'm proud of you." Gideon offered him a smile.

Austin didn't return it. He turned his angry, hard gaze on Gideon instead. "You don't have any right to feel that way about me."

Gideon's time of reckoning had come much sooner than he anticipated. "You don't understand."

The hurt and anger that contorted Austin's face almost took Gideon's breath away. It was so raw, like a gaping, bleeding wound.

"You don't think I understand? My brother was dead, and the one person I trusted, the one other person in the whole fucking world who might have understood me, left without a fucking word. No phone calls. No texts. Not even a fucking email. I had to carry that devastation alone when I could have carried it with you." Austin's hands were out of his pockets, fisted at his sides. He was practically vibrating with rage, pink color high on his cheeks. His voice had been modulated, tightly controlled, and at odds with his body language.

Gideon wished Austin would yell. If that's what it took to satisfy Austin, Gideon would even take a punch. He deserved it.

Gideon fell to his knees. He was used to kneeling; it was a standard position to take when giving a confession. And what was this if not a confession?

He balled his fists on his thighs. The floor was hard on his bones.

The sudden movement startled Austin, who took a step back. "What are you doing?"

"It was my fault."

Austin's brow furrowed, the long stems of his roses almost meeting. "What the fuck are you talking about?"

Gideon clenched his fists, closing his eyes against Austin's face. "It was my fault." His voice was a ragged rasp across his vocal cords, but he could do this. He had to. He had done it once; he had confessed to his mentor in seminary, who understood his need for penance, for atonement. "It was my fault. I convinced Luke to cut third period and go off campus for lunch. That's why we were in the lobby when ... when it happened."

It had been some white kid Gideon didn't know. Some sophomore with his dad's automatic rifle. He'd looked surprised to see Gideon and Luke walk through the front doors, probably because they weren't supposed to be there. They'd surprised him, startled him maybe.

They weren't his original targets, just the most convenient.

Luke had walked in the door first, in front of Gideon. It could have so easily been him instead.

Gideon couldn't remember how he'd ended up on the floor—whether he'd fallen on purpose or by accident, or whether the weight of Luke's body had dragged him down. That was one detail that always eluded him.

He could always remember the heat of Luke's blood on his face.

The sound his mother made when she found out.

The eyes of all those people at Luke's funeral.

The fact that Luke's parents had to cremate him because there wasn't enough left of his chest for a casket.

There wasn't enough room in Gideon's head or heart for the horrors of it all.

A hand landed on his shoulder, thumb digging into his clavicle. The grip was hard and painful, but it was also good and grounding.

"You let that go," Austin demanded fiercely. "I can blame you for leaving, but I *never*—not once, ever—blamed you for his death, Gideon. You fucking let that go." Austin gave him a little shake.

Gideon couldn't let it go, though. It was a piece of the fabric of his soul, tangled up with all the rest of himself. It was a burden he carried. His cross, his cup.

He found himself shaking his head.

No. No, he wouldn't.

"Let it go." Austin squeezed tighter, so hard that Gideon gasped.

Another shake.

Austin's body heat washed over Gideon; his eyes were clamped tightly shut, but he felt Austin kneel in front of him, so close their knees touched. Too close.

"Look at me."

That was another thing Gideon found himself incapable of doing.

Austin lifted his hand off Gideon's shoulder then used both to grab either side of Gideon's face, thumbs pressing into his cheeks. "Look at me, Gideon Gray."

Gideon did.

Austin's stormy eyes were glassy. Moisture clung to his dark lashes, but his mouth was hard and determined. "You know whose fault it was? That fucking kid's. If he hadn't shot himself, I would have killed him myself for what he did. Do you understand me?" Austin gave Gideon's face a small shake.

"You can't think like that," Gideon finally said because he didn't want Austin to carry that hate. He had done nothing but lost everything.

"I do. Sometimes, I do." The pads of his thumbs softly brushed across Gideon's cheeks. "You have to let it go."

Then Austin kissed him, and Gideon fell apart all over again.

# CHAPTER FOUR
## AUSTIN

Austin didn't know what the fuck he was doing.

He hadn't consciously made the decision to kiss Gideon. But he'd just looked so devastated, spouting off some bullshit about how Luke's death was his fault. Austin had blamed a lot of people over the years, but Gideon had never been one of them.

Then, there was the fact that Gideon was on his knees in front of him, and Austin didn't know what to do with the feelings that had bubbled up inside him at the sight. Gideon was an imposing figure, broad and a couple of inches taller than Austin. Seeing such a man on his fucking knees had rearranged his insides and made his cock hard.

Gideon had looked up at him with those sad eyes and plush lips, and Austin just wanted to make it better.

It was irrational, inappropriate, and probably immoral. Gideon was the epitome of off-limits ... and yet Austin had done it anyway.

He always had been an unrepentant fuckboy.

A flush crept up Gideon's neck, and his mouth gaped slightly. There was a small divot bisecting his plump lower lip that made Austin itch to bite it.

Austin rubbed the pads of his thumbs over the sweet arches of Gideon's cheek bones. Gideon was breathing hard, his chest almost touching Austin's with every inhale.

"Let it go, Gideon."

Gideon finally opened his eyes, and the sight almost stopped Austin's heart. Gideon's regard was heated but tortured. Conflicted, and filled with a kind of deep guilt and desperation that Austin would probably never be able to understand.

The blue of Gideon's eyes had turned stormy, the air between the men so charged that Austin was surprised there were no sparks.

They still had so much to talk about. Austin still had so many questions Gideon needed to answer for. But he wanted to ease a bit of the pain that shone so freely on Gideon's face. Take some of the burden, bear some of the guilt.

Austin slid a hand to the back of Gideon's neck and gently squeezed.

Gideon gasped, lips parting in invitation. In temptation.

"I'm going to kiss you," Austin said, squeezing again. "If
you don't want that, I need you to say so."

Gideon said nothing. He just stared at Austin with those
thunderclap eyes, his pulse hammering under Austin's
palm and hands clenched on his thighs.

Austin leaned forward, moving inexorably slowly to give
Gideon time to change his mind. When there was less than
a breath between their mouths, Austin paused, closed his
eyes, and waited.

Gideon's sigh brushed across his lips.

Then Austin felt the barest of touches as Gideon closed
the distance between them.

The kiss was slow and experimental, tentative and tor-
turous in equal measure. Austin's hand flexed on Gideon's
nape, and Gideon groaned. Austin licked at Gideon's lips,
pressing against the seam of his mouth, teasing him softly.

Gideon opened with a ragged exhale.

Austin's heart leapt in his chest, even as his dick hard-
ened in his jeans. He shoved his hand roughly into the curls
on the back of Gideon's head and plunged his tongue into
Gideon's mouth.

Gideon was nothing but soft shoulders and pliant lips
under Austin's hands and mouth. It made Austin feel feral
and uncontrolled and untamed.

He roughened the kiss, nipping at Gideon's lips, choking him on his tongue. Gideon whined, his hands clutching at Austin's hips.

Austin wanted to touch him, see if Gideon's skin was as soft as his sweet mouth or the little sounds he made in the back of his throat.

Austin tugged his head back so he could lick at the line of Gideon's jaw and the hard column of his throat. The fine blond stubble, barely visible in the light, rasped across Austin's sensitive skin and sent a bolt of fire down his spine.

Gideon was putty in Austin's hands. His breath hitched when Austin sucked on his pulse.

Austin used his hold on Gideon's curls to crash their mouths together again, Gideon's tongue tangling with his.

Gideon let out a small whine when Austin pulled away again.

Austin tightened his hold on Gideon's hair. He liked the way tendons in Gideon's neck strained. "Such a hot mouth, Father."

They both froze as if surprised by what Austin had just said. But Austin didn't care because he'd meant every word. Gideon's lips were wet and swollen from Austin's attention, and it just made him want those lips wrapped around his dick.

How pretty Gideon would be then.

Then Gideon did something unexpected. The corner of his mouth tipped up in a small, quiet smile. Gideon's blistering fingers stole under Austin's shirt. "You shouldn't remind me of all the vows I'm breaking when I'm kissing you."

Austin snorted. "I'll shut up then."

Their mouths crashed together again. This time, Gideon fought him for control of the kiss, his large hands spanning Austin's waist and mashing their hips together.

Gideon was stiff and hot in his austere black slacks.

Austin trailed his open palm down the center of Gideon's hard chest and taut stomach, and palmed his erection. Gideon shuddered. Austin's fingers were deft on the buttons until he'd freed Gideon's cock.

Fuck, the man was huge. Austin's throat went a little dry as he imagined what it might be like to choke on Gideon's dick.

Gideon moaned and pressed his face into Austin's neck as Austin's fingers wrapped around his shaft. He rubbed his thumb through the precum gathered at the tip, pressing gently into Gideon's slit.

Gideon's teeth scraped along the skin of Austin's throat. Austin stroked the shaft, squeezing gently, enjoying the way Gideon's hips thrust into his touch.

Austin moved down, leisurely exploring the girth of the man, the coarse dark curls at his base, his balls, and the delicate skin of his taint.

Gideon inhaled sharply when the pad of Austin's forefinger brushed across his asshole. Pain registered as Gideon's fingers dug into Austin's hips.

"I'm not going to last long if you do that."

Austin dragged his fingers back to Gideon's shaft, and he sighed, even as Austin tugged roughly on his cock.

"Good," Austin said.

His own need was burning and demanding in his balls and his spine, but he wanted to get Gideon off first.

He wanted to ruin him.

He wanted to save him.

He wanted things he couldn't say.

So, he jacked Gideon until the bigger man was shuddering and panting, and nipping at Austin's bottom lip.

Hot semen spilled across Austin's fingers, feeling like a sear against the skin of his wrist.

# CHAPTER FIVE

# GIDEON

Gideon was supposed to be listening to the updates from the fall festival committee chair, but he couldn't think of anything except Austin.

Austin's mouth.

Austin's tongue.

Austin's hand on Gideon's dick.

How was he supposed to lead Mass on Sunday when his blood heated every time he saw the altar where he'd been on his knees?

He hadn't touched a man since he'd taken his final vows; he hadn't lied when he told Austin it had been a long time for him. And now, he felt insatiable.

He expected to feel some kind of guilt, but it didn't come. Maybe he was too full of guilt already for one little broken vow to mean much.

The committee chair was a middle-aged white woman whose two kids attended youth group and all the church's other extracurricular activities. Gideon was sure they would be volunteers for the fall festival too.

Paige. Her name was Paige, and she was nice enough. Organized. She had a hot-pink leather planner spread open across Gideon's desk in the parish office. She had lists and charts, and a map of the church's parking lot.

That's really the only reason Gideon was being consulted; he really didn't have much to offer in the way of event planning, but the festival was held in St. Benedict's parking lot, so he was consulted out of courtesy.

He was sure Paige had everything under control.

"Do we have an organization picked out yet? For the donation?" he asked.

Paige stuttered to a halt in the middle of her sentence. She blinked owlishly at him. Gideon must have not been paying attention to the thread of the conversation.

"Oh, umm ..." Paige thumbed through some of her notes. The festival was a community fundraising project, and they usually picked a local organization to partner with. "The committee was thinking about the teen youth group this year. Maybe we could raise enough to take the kids on a mission—"

"No," Gideon interrupted, a bit more brusquely than he usually would. "The youth group has enough money. And if they want to do service projects, there's plenty to be done here."

He *detested* mission trips.

Paige's face turned a bit red. She was flustered but pushed through. "Oh, well, we still have time to finalize that. The committee has a list, and we've had some organizations reach out. The real issue is that we've lost one of the vendor booths." She whipped out a seating chart. "They weren't really interested in our profit-sharing philosophy."

She handed the paper to Gideon, and the tone of her voice made it very clear what she thought of the vendor who'd backed out, leaving an embarrassing blank spot on her map.

Gideon ran a hand thoughtfully over the light stubble on his jaw. "Can you fill it?"

Paige huffed. "It'll be hard but not impossible. We're only two weeks out. A lot of people are going to be booked and won't be able to show up at the last minute."

Gideon let the paper flutter back down on the desk. "Give me the afternoon. I have an idea."

The idea had come to him fully formed as soon as he saw the blank space on Paige's carefully labeled map.

It was purely for selfish reasons.

He wasn't sure if he was supposed to see Austin again; they hadn't spoken about it. Maybe that one quick little encounter was enough for him.

But it wasn't enough for Gideon.

He wasn't supposed to *want*. He wasn't supposed to covet. But he did. He wanted and he desired and he coveted his dead best friend's little brother.

Gideon wasn't sold on the idea of hell. He never had been. Even after his Master of Divinity and propaedeutic year, he was not sold on eternal damnation as punishment for his sins.

There were only some people he wished a hell upon.

And he was not one of them. Neither was Austin.

Sabbath Ink was easy to find. You couldn't miss it from the road. It was a squat square building with a large parking lot that was mostly empty. But Gideon assumed he wasn't showing up during prime tattooing hours.

The entrance to the shop was decorated with hay bales, pumpkins, and corn stalks, and a little bell tinkled when he walked in.

He was greeted at the door by a petite Black woman in sky-high heels and bright-blue lipstick.

She eyed his black suit and white collar, and one sharp eyebrow rose skeptically. "Can I help you?"

Gideon suddenly wished he had changed into his civilian clothes. But he had been in such a rush. He tried to keep the embarrassment from showing on his face. "Is Austin here?"

He realized that, even as the owner, Austin could have days off like everyone else. Then what would Gideon do next?

The woman frowned slightly, and then she walked towards the back and hollered, "Austin, there's a priest here for you. What the hell did you do now?"

Austin appeared quickly. At first, his eyes widened with shock, and then his mouth curled up in a sly grin. "Thanks, Niyah."

The woman nodded and went back to her day, giving them an illusion of privacy.

Austin leaned an elbow on the front desk. "What can I do for you, Father?" he drawled, every word laced with suggestion.

He was wearing a loose button-up floral shirt and a pair of scandalously short shorts, which put most of his lean legs on display.

Gideon tried not to leer at all the exposed skin or the colorful leaves, vines, and insects wrapping around each thigh. Judging by the little smirk on Austin's face, he'd failed.

"I need a favor," Gideon said with no preamble.

Austin's eyes sparkled, and he tugged on his bottom lip with his teeth. "I love doing favors."

Gideon could feel the heat on his face, crawling up his neck. "I have an empty spot at the church's fall festival, and I was hoping you could fill it. I know it's short notice, but I'm sure I could find someone to help with supplies if you need it." And now he was rambling.

Austin's brow furrowed. "You want me to tattoo at a festival?"

Well, Gideon understood the confusion. He should have been clearer. "No, I was thinking face painting or something."

"You want me to paint the faces of ... the children?" Austin sounded like he was trying not to laugh.

"Mostly kids, yes," Gideon said.

Austin looked at him, a thoughtful tilt to his brows, his gaze raking Gideon from head to toe. Gideon tried not to fidget. He took it as a good sign that Austin hadn't just rejected the idea outright.

Austin grinned. "I'll do that for you, but you have to do something for me too."

Heat curled immediately around Gideon's spine. He fought to keep his face neutral and his voice steady. "What is it?"

Austin glanced over his shoulder before grabbing a Sharpie from a collection of pens on the counter. Then he took hold of Gideon's hand and turned it. "Come to my apartment tonight, about midnight." He scrawled an address across the middle of Gideon's palm.

Gideon gently curled his fingers around the information, heart pounding in his throat.

Austin stepped closer, fingers still wrapped around Gideon's wrist. "And bring your safeword." Austin winked.

Emotion stabbed through Gideon's chest. It still wasn't guilt, more like ... disappointment, he guessed. It wasn't like he could date Austin. Gideon had vowed to be alone for the rest of his life. He was supposed to be married to his church, his parish, his god.

He could only steal glances and moments with Austin under the cover of darkness.

That's all he could have, all he could give, and he should be thankful Austin even wanted to see him again.

Gideon told Paige that Sabbath Ink would be filling her missing spot, then retired to the rectory and changed into a long-sleeved tee and jeans to wait until midnight.

He tried to do other things, like finish the biography he was currently reading or the sci-fi novel. Maybe write his homily for the next Sunday. Or even wash Austin's address off his hand and scrub the man from his memory and thoughts.

But he was stuck.

For the first time in years, he was feeling something other than numb apathy, crippling guilt, or hot fury.

Sometimes, the anger hit him out of nowhere, so hard and so fast that he felt like puking. Then he had thoughts like Austin—that he would kill that boy for what he'd done if he could. Then he had to go to confession at the church a town over and recite five Hail Marys.

The apathy, the nothingness, was better.

The small seed of hope that had taken root in his chest was painful.

He should have left his encounter with Austin, on the floor of his church, as just that—one single luminous moment in time, a memory that could sustain him for years.

Instead, he showed up at the address Austin had scrawled onto his skin.

The apartment complex was only a few minutes up the road, right off of Main Street. Maybe if it had been farther away, Gideon would have found more self-control.

He knocked.

A grinning Austin greeted him at the door. "You're punctual," he said, leading Gideon into the apartment.

It was a studio, neat and moody, with most of the furniture in dark colors or rustic wood. There was a desk area, a drawing table, records and posters on the walls.

Gideon tried not to let his eyes wander towards the bed. It was large, with navy and burnt-orange pillow cases. There were also a surprising number of house plants scattered around, which Gideon found endearing—not that he needed another excuse to like Austin.

Austin walked towards a door that must lead to the bathroom, tugging his shirt over his head and dropping it haphazardly on the floor. "You don't mind if I shower?" He threw another charming, boyish grin over his lean shoulder.

Gideon shook his head, leaning his back against the front door. His throat went dry when he caught a glimpse of firm ass cheek since Austin kept shedding clothes before he disappeared.

Gideon wasn't some blushing virgin. He'd fucked his way through college indiscriminately. He was coping in the only way he knew how.

He knew why he was here, why he'd come.

A puff of steam preceded Austin's exit from the bathroom ... and he was completely naked.

Gideon shouldn't have been shocked, but he had expected more ... overture. He tried to remember to breathe.

Austin looked like he could have been carved from marble by some ancient Greek, like a young demigod. Or even a few centuries later, Le Genie du Maal. The Lucifer that was too hot for church.

Austin's body was soft, his muscles long and sinewy under his skin, hips and waist slender, and thighs and calves supple and round. His cock was already semihard, hanging proudly between his legs, nestled in neat dark hair.

Damp hair coiled on Austin's forehead and over the tops of his ears. "Did you do what I told you to?"

"What?" Gideon's reply was a strangled gasp.

Austin padded closer, and Gideon's heart thumped in time with his footsteps.

Austin grabbed Gideon's jaw. His brow arched. "Are you being difficult already?" His thumb brushed across Gideon's bottom lip. "Your safeword, baby."

Gideon was barely breathing anymore. "'Sacrament'."

A muscle fluttered in Austin's jaw. "Do you know how this works?"

Gideon nodded, his whole body aching to take whatever Austin wanted to give.

The fingers on his jaw tightened.

"You're going to let me do whatever I want with you, right? If it gets to be too much, you'll use your word and everything stops."

Gideon nodded again.

"I need to hear you say it."

Gideon's breath rattled out. "Yes."

Something slid into place inside Gideon's mind. He was relinquishing control to Austin. He could just *be*. He could just *feel*. He didn't have to *think*.

Austin's hand slid from Gideon's jaw to his shoulder. He didn't exert any extra pressure, but Gideon felt the weight of that hand echo through his entire being.

The side of Austin's mouth tipped up. "Then get on your knees, Father."

Gideon did as he was told, his hands skimming down Austin's bare flanks, until his knees hit the floor. He was level with Austin's bobbing dick, but he didn't dare touch him. Not yet.

Austin let out a breathy laugh. "You're a fast learner." He leaned his hips slightly forward so that the tip of his cock brushed over Gideon's closed mouth.

But Gideon had gotten a feel for the game now. He didn't move. He didn't open his mouth.

"Good boy," Austin purred, his voice sensual and slick, the tight hand in Gideon's curls betraying his desire. "Now, show me how much you want me."

Gideon sighed, his warm breath causing Austin's cock to twitch.

Gideon ran his palms up the lean lines of Austin's thighs, enjoying the way the muscles jumped under his touch. Austin's skin smelled like fresh soap, like an afternoon after a spring rain.

Austin's cock was hot and hard, skin stretched tight, the head swollen and dripping. Gideon kissed the tip with exquisite tenderness, and Austin sucked in a sharp breath.

Gideon peppered soft kisses down the shaft, one of his hands cupping Austin's rounded ass while the other slid around his hip.

Austin cursed when Gideon finally took him in his mouth. Gideon sucked and relaxed his throat as much as he could, his heart beating wildly as Austin thrust into his mouth.

He heard two thuds as Austin slammed his hands against the door to brace himself. Gideon drew away, laving his tongue over the head, sucking at it, teasing it with his teeth, and dipping into the slit.

Austin panted above him. "Fuck, Gideon. Fuck, fuck."

Everything about Gideon was aching—his thighs, his balls, his jaw, his chest—but he sucked Austin back down his throat.

Austin thrusted again, and Gideon let his body go soft, encouraging the movement without words since his mouth was full. He squeezed Austin's ass, fingertips drifting into the cleft.

"Fuck, baby. I'm gonna come down that greedy little throat." Austin's words were a ragged drawl as he bucked his hips.

Austin's muscles flexed and quivered under Gideon's hands, and Gideon knew the man was close. With a shudder and a rough exhalation, Austin finished, hot semen spurting down Gideon's throat.

He swallowed furiously, but some still spilled out of the sides of his mouth. Austin pulled back, the abrupt movement causing more cum to drip down Gideon's chin, onto his clean shirt.

Austin didn't seem to mind. His eyes glittered as his fingers touched Gideon's lips, spreading the cum around his face. He plucked at the collar of Gideon's shirt. "Oh, you've made such a mess."

# Chapter Six

## Austin

Austin had never seen anything as pretty as Gideon on his knees with cum on his face. His cheeks were flushed, big blue eyes glassy and brimming, chest rising and falling with rapid breaths.

He looked different tonight than he had on the floor of the church. His body was looser and thighs splayed farther apart than before. Regular clothes made him appear boyish, even though he was only in his early thirties.

The shirt left the column of his throat exposed. Austin could see the little hollow between his collar bones.

Austin didn't know a damn thing about religion, God, or sin. He knew about art, color theory, and want. He wanted Gideon Gray so badly it felt like a yawning, empty chasm in his chest. A hole that would never be filled.

Had he always felt this way, or was it new?

With his balls aching, and his cock quickly hardening again just from watching Gideon, he could save that conundrum for another day.

"You're overdressed," he said, working hard to keep his tone high and haughty. He was supposed to be the one in charge here—for now. He wanted to conquer but also submit. The two feelings warred inside him, making it hard to concentrate.

Gideon inhaled a shaky breath. He started with the hem of his shirt, slowly pulling the fabric up the cut lines of his abdomen. Pectoral muscles flexed and shifted as he lifted the shirt off his head and tossed it casually away.

Gideon held Austin's eyes as his hands moved to the button on his jeans and the zipper.

Austin's lungs ached, and he knew he was holding his breath. He had felt Gideon's dick but had not laid eyes on it yet. Seeing him naked, stripped down, felt like something ... transcendent.

Gideon had to stand to get the jeans off his hips. The front gaped open, exposing black boxers and a considerable erection. He shed his shoes and socks, then jeans and underwear, the clothes stacking up in a discarded pile.

The soft lighting of Austin's apartment made Gideon look like a god, with his golden hair and golden skin and golden trail of hair.

Austin forgot himself for a moment, forgot what he wanted so desperately to do to Gideon. He took a breath, settling himself back in his skin, in his role, and watched Gideon's plush mouth tip up on one side.

Gideon wouldn't be amused in a minute. He'd be desperate and writhing.

Austin, despite his current urges—Gideon was naked and leaking right in front of him—took several steps back until the edge of his bed brushed his calf.

"Come here," he said.

Gideon did as he was told, padding forward. His footfalls were quiet and graceful, unobtrusive. Austin took a few more steps backward, and Gideon followed, keeping the space between their bodies even.

They were facing each other at the end of Austin's bed.

Austin's hand dangled by his side, fingers running over the lengths of bright-red rope he had carefully folded on the bed.

Gideon's eyes followed his movements, widening slightly.

"Is it too much?"

"I'll tell you when it's too much," Gideon said, voice breathless but firm.

Austin brushed his knuckles across Gideon's. "I'm going to tie you up." He grabbed Gideon's shaft and squeezed. The skin was taut and hot. Color was high on Gideon's cheeks. "Then I'll let you come."

Last year, an ex had taken Austin to a Shibari demonstration at a kink club out of state. He'd become obsessed immediately with the press of rope on skin, the marks left behind in flesh.

A shiver slid down his spine.

He wasn't talented enough yet for any suspension, but he had mastered most of the basic chest, arm, and body holds.

Gideon stepped forward, and their chests touched, cocks sliding together. Gideon grabbed his jaw and crashed their mouths together for a quick, scorching, desperate kiss that had his breathing shuddering and limbs tingling with anticipation.

Austin broke the kiss with a grin. "Hands behind your back."

Gideon bowed his head so blond curls fell across his face. His eyes were closed, mouth soft, and expression serene—almost like he was in prayer.

Austin adjusted his arms so they were in the proper position—one on top of the other, palms up—so Gideon could grasp each opposite forearm after he was bound.

Austin started to weave the ropes around Gideon's chest, laying the rope under and around his pectorals. He worked in silence, except for the sound of ragged breathing. Gideon held his position while Austin tested knots and pressure, ensuring it wasn't too constricting against Gideon's skin. The back of his knuckles brushed against

Gideon as he worked, leaving a trail of warmth and red blush in his wake.

When he was finished, Gideon's wrists were bound together, resting in the small of his back; there was a large knot nestled in the hollow of his throat, and ropes criss-crossed his torso in a large diamond.

"Bend over." Austin's voice had gone rough. He tipped his chin towards the bed.

Gideon was surprisingly graceful, hoisting himself up to a kneeling position at the end of the bed with his arms bound. Austin's fingertips brushed Gideon's bare hips, just in case there was any wobble or sway, but the man had a core of steel.

Gideon braced himself on the firm mattress, thighs splayed. His breath hitched as Austin's hands traveled over his hips and down his thick thighs. Austin pressed gently on the small of Gideon's back, and Gideon responded to the silent command like he'd been born to it.

He leaned forward, his torso gently lowering to the bed, ass rising. Austin's dick spasmed. Words stuck in his dry throat.

Gideon was fucking exquisite.

Austin ran his hands over Gideon's ass; it was split like a perfect round peach. Austin gripped his hips and ran his cock through the cleft. They groaned in unison.

Austin's fingers dug into Gideon's skin. "Are you here for atonement? Forgiveness?"

Gideon's fingers twitched, and he inhaled a deep breath. "Yes."

Austin stroked the soft, unblemished, unmarked skin of one cheek. "I think you need to be punished."

Gideon's whole body quivered under his hand. There was a soft, "Yes."

Austin's reply was just as soft. "That's what I thought."

He started with a soft swat, almost gentle, just to see how Gideon would react. He moaned softly, so Austin repeated the action, increasing the pressure until Gideon's skin turned red. Then he switched to the other cheek.

He was only a couple of passes in when a roughened sound left Gideon's throat. His hips bucked, and Austin realized quickly what had happened.

"Oh, baby." He reached between their bodies to grab Gideon's cock and pump him through the rest of his orgasm. Austin gathered cum on his fingers and brought them back to Gideon's tight little hole. He spread the cum between his flamed and reddened cheeks.

He pressed the pad of his thumb to the hole, and Gideon let out a strangled sound, his shoulders straining against the ropes.

Austin had one mildly terrifying thought. "You're not ..."

Gideon laughed softly, even as his hips pushed back against Austin's hands. "I'm celibate, not a virgin, Austin."

What a relief. Austin would be gentle with him but not *that* gentle.

He stroked down Gideon's spine, pressing their bodies together so he could feel the heat from his spanking.

Austin had a bottle of lube on standby, but he liked the idea of opening Gideon up with his own cum.

Austin worked his thumb around the delicate skin, pressing inside and feeling Gideon's muscles push back. He switched to his forefinger, pushing against Gideon's entrance, stroking his back with his other hand. Gideon's hips quivered, and the desperate little sounds he made sent fire to Austin's engorged dick.

"Let me in, baby," he purred.

Gideon whimpered, his thighs falling further apart. Austin's finger breached him completely.

Austin worked him until he felt confident he could add another finger. "Good boy. You're doing such a great job getting this greedy hole ready for me. You're gonna take my cock like this, aren't you? Suck it all down?"

Gideon moaned loudly, the sound strangled in his throat, his muscles fluttering over Austin's fingers.

Austin was so hard he felt like he might just go blind from the pressure. He needed to be inside Gideon's body. Judging by the way Gideon was grasping at Austin's fingers, he was ready enough.

Austin withdrew, rubbing small circles on Gideon's hip. "Condom or no condom?" His voice was strange and jagged to his own ears.

"God, none." Gideon's voice trembled. "There's been no one else in … years."

"Fuck yes."

If Austin was a religious man, he might have sent a quick prayer of thanks to whatever god had sent him someone as perfect as Gideon Gray.

Austin grabbed the lube, dripping dollops onto Gideon's ass so that they trickled down his crevice. Gideon flinched and gasped at the cool liquid hitting his overheated skin.

Austin used the tip of his dick to spread the lube, pressing gently inside, the tightness constricting his lungs. "So fucking perfect, Gray."

# CHAPTER SEVEN
## GIDEON

Gideon was overrun with sensations.

His body was riddled with aches that were new and delicious. His shoulders, arms, and chest ached from the ropes, his ass from Austin's spanking, and his entrance from Austin's slow invasion. The tip of his cock, where it bobbed across Austin's bedding, begged for relief. He was hard again but could do nothing about it.

Then there was the smell of Austin's sheets underneath him. In his prone position, Gideon couldn't escape the clean scent of Austin's skin or the spicy hints of his cologne.

Gideon struggled against his bindings; he wanted to touch himself. He wanted to touch Austin. But he could only lie there and take what he was given.

Gideon bucked his hips into Austin's. "Harder." He gasped. "I want to feel you in the morning."

Austin grunted, his fingertips tightening on Gideon's hips. Gideon sucked in a sharp breath as Austin drove into him even deeper than before. Pleasure skittered up and down Gideon's limbs; his cock leaked, making an even bigger mess on the sheets.

If he were a better man, he may have had room in his head for thoughts about the vow he was breaking. He may have cared. But the only thing he could think of was how full he felt, how perfect and right Austin's body felt pounding against his.

Gideon hissed as Austin grabbed his cock, pumping him in time with his driving thrusts. It wasn't gentle. It wasn't sweet. It was something ethereal, something cleansing. The pain and the pleasure, and the scrape of the rope chased away the demons that always dogged him.

"Fuck." Austin grunted, his hips stuttering. "You're so tight, baby. So good for me. I'm going to fill you up. Are you going to come with me?"

Gideon was. Hot fire ripped through his body.

Austin throbbed inside him. A few final pumps, and then he was gone, and Gideon wanted to protest at the loss. He wasn't ready to feel empty again.

He immediately missed the heft and warmth of Austin's body, but Austin's hands worked on the knots that bound him. Then, there was a tingling rush of blood as the ropes fell away from Gideon's biceps.

Gideon could only lie there, in a sweet, numbed-out state of bliss, as Austin puttered around the apartment doing God knows what.

Austin returned, sitting on the edge of the bed, his lower half covered by a pair of baggy basketball shorts. He rubbed a hand through Gideon's sweaty hair. "How are you feeling?"

Gideon gave him what was certainly a loopy grin. "Used."

Austin huffed a laugh, his neck pinking. "Here, hydrate."

Gideon did what he could to prop himself up on one elbow, the red ropes falling off around him, and took the bottle of water Austin offered.

He drank and watched Austin's eyes travel over the marks indented in his skin.

Austin swallowed. "Scootch," he ordered.

Gideon rolled himself up onto the pillows, and Austin laid a towel over the not-insignificant mess they'd made at the end of the bed.

He pushed the red ropes off the end unceremoniously and crawled up beside Gideon, adopting the same bent-elbow pose so that they were facing each other. "Shower or food first?"

Gideon laughed. "It's late. Where would we get food?"

"Leave that to me, baby. My shower is only big enough for one—I know because I've tried—so why don't you shower, and I'll heat you up a plate?" He leaned forward and pecked Gideon on the nose, and Gideon's heart did weird things in his chest.

Like a zombie, Gideon found his way into Austin's bathroom. He had been right; the bathroom was size-appropriate for the studio apartment, which meant it was tiny. You could sit on the toilet and touch the pedestal vanity and the shower curtain.

He caught a glimpse of his messy, disheveled red face in the mirror before he turned the shower on.

He hadn't come prepared to stay the night. That wasn't what they were doing, right? That's not what Austin wanted, did he?

Gideon showered quickly, feeling some kind of way as he ran soapy hands over the fading rope marks on his arms, washing Austin's spend off his thighs.

He had no clothes, so Gideon just wrapped a spare towel around his waist.

Austin was in the small kitchen area when he came back into the room, making what looked like two plates of spaghetti.

Gideon slid onto one of the bar chairs at the island.

"Voilà." Austin sat one of the plates in front of him. "Homemade baked spaghetti. Well, leftover homemade baked spaghetti."

Gideon suddenly found that he was ravenous. He dug into his portion and was halfway through before he stopped for air. "It's really good," he said.

Austin was eating his spaghetti in measured bites. "Greedy in all things, I see."

Gideon flushed. "I didn't know you were such a cook." But he guessed he didn't know much about the adult version of Austin at all.

Austin leaned a hip against the island. "Do you remember when you and Luke tried to help me with a science project and singed my eyebrows off? My mom was so pissed. Mostly about the chaos we'd made in the kitchen but also because it was right before picture day."

Gideon's throat constricted. Austin had a small, wistful smile on his face as he pushed around another bite.

Gideon wondered what had prompted the memory. He tried to remember exactly the moment Austin had referred to. It had been a project for the science fair in middle school. They wanted to build an exploding volcano because all the best science projects actually exploded. It had taken forever for Austin's eyebrows to grow back.

Austin's fork clanged against the plate. "It's hard to talk about him but hard not to talk about him, you know?"

Gideon nodded. He knew. Sometimes, it felt like Luke had just disappeared when they were seventeen, and Gideon could just leave all those golden memories alone, preserved but fading. Sometimes, he could pretend Luke hadn't died horrifically.

Austin was the only person in the world who could have the same feelings.

"I didn't mean it before," Austin said. "About being forgiven. It was just, you know, sex talk."

Gideon swallowed. "Most of the time, I think I do need to ... be forgiven."

Austin snorted. "That's the survivor's guilt talking. Did you not get therapy? I had *so* much therapy."

Gideon finished his plate at a more moderate speed to stall for some time to collect his thoughts. "I did, a little bit. But it was lackluster. I was young and in college, and there were better things to do to forget."

He had shown up for a couple of free sessions at the university's counseling center, but he didn't fully buy into their code of anonymity and was afraid to be overly honest with his counselor—a young woman who'd barely looked older than him. He was afraid to tell her what he really thought, what he really felt, in case she decided she needed to tell someone else.

Austin grinned at him. "Not always so devout then?"

"No, not always. That came later." He cleared his throat. "I was very much your typical college student." Plus, the traumatic backstory.

"But you quit baseball."

"I quit baseball."

Both he and Luke had already committed to play for LSU on full scholarships. Then Luke died. And Gideon couldn't go play baseball on a team without him.

The athletic director had sent flowers to Luke's funeral and a card to Luke's mom. He didn't understand Gideon's decision; no one did.

Austin grabbed both of their plates, spraying them with the dish soap that sat next to the sink, and started running a stream of hot water into the bowl.

"Then what?" Austin prodded. Dishes clinked. "How did you go from average college student to pious man of the cloth?" Austin poked a soapy fork in his direction. "For a religion that hates us, I might add."

For Gideon, it wasn't about the specific denomination or even God. He was drawn to the history, the ceremony, the drama and ritual of Catholicism. He was well aware of the failures and injustices of the Catholic Church. That's why he tried to do good. How could he explain his ever-present search for meaning? For penance? For an explanation for why a god would take away his best friend in such a way?

Maybe he felt like he didn't deserve nice things to happen to him. Maybe he wanted to be walled off behind a vow and a white collar. Maybe he wanted to be alone.

Even as he thought it, he knew it wasn't true.

The feelings he had when he was with Austin were not the feelings of a man who wanted to be alone.

Gideon cleared his throat. He owed Austin this, at least.

"At first, it was psychology. I was bound and determined to figure out why he'd done it. I wanted to understand. But it turned out that wasn't enough. It wasn't enough to understand the why in such a clinical way." Gideon rubbed his palms on his thighs. He wasn't looking at Austin anymore, so he couldn't see his reactions. He stared at the marbling on the island instead. "I wanted to know why Luke. Why him and not me."

Austin was there, nudging between his thighs and cupping his face in his hands again. "Nobody can answer that, Gideon. Not even God."

"It should have been me. It would have been easier if it had been me." Gideon wasn't close to his family. His father had lost interest once he found out Gideon wouldn't play college ball. He had no siblings. The Davenports had been his family.

"Do you really think Luke would have been okay if it was you?"

Gideon's chest felt like it was cracking wide open. "You would have been okay."

Austin kissed him on the lips, but the kiss lacked heat. It was chaste and sweet, the barest brush of his lips. "If you think that, you've really lost your damn mind."

Gideon looped his arms around Austin's slender waist, pulling him close until they were bare chest to bare chest.

Austin's heat sunk into his skin. He huffed a chuckle, the air stirring the top of Gideon's curls.

Maybe Gideon could stay wrapped in Austin's arms forever, safe in his apartment—this liminal space that felt removed from his regular life. From his duties, his responsibilities, his parishioners. From his guilt, his shame.

*Impossible.*

The feelings crawling through his gut were impossible. He couldn't have what Austin was offering with his soft lips and firm arms.

Gideon couldn't have his peace.

# CHAPTER EIGHT

## AUSTIN

Something was wrong.

Well, something other than the fact that he'd fucked his brother's best friend who also happened to be an ordained priest.

Something other than *that*.

Austin didn't know what he was expecting, but being ghosted wasn't one of the options he'd considered.

He should have, though, because it's not like he could date a priest.

Gideon had left his apartment in the early morning hours, and he hadn't heard from him since.

Maybe he was busy.

Maybe he had come to his senses in a way Austin had not.

Maybe the fall festival or fundraiser, or whatever the hell it was, took up a lot of time.

Austin had felt something during their moment in the kitchen, when Gideon had hugged him, burying his nose in his throat and holding onto Austin like his life depended on it. Surely, Gideon had felt it too?

"Are you smoking pot again?" Niyah's voice cut through his somber musings.

"What?"

"You're totally zoned out."

Austin's elbow, where he leaned over the front counter, slipped a bit. He had just been staring out into space with his chin propped in his hand. "I'm thinking."

"That's new."

"Har har." Austin shuffled papers across the desk with one finger. He assumed they were what Niyah wanted to talk about.

"So, I don't really know much about children, but these are the design options I think would work best." She slid a piece of paper in his eye line. "Very on theme."

They were. Pumpkins, some leaves, a cute cup of hot chocolate with marshmallows. Then there were some kid-friendly staples: rainbows, butterflies, snakes, and a mermaid tail. They were all easy enough for Austin to do in a couple of minutes and with a few colors.

"If you feel like getting really wild, you can do something like this." She pushed more paper in front of him, and instead of little designs that could be done on cheeks, there were examples of half-face masks that were still mostly butterfly wings.

"Yeah, looks good."

Niyah frowned at him, clearly displeased. "This is so far outside of my job description, so the least *you* could do is show a little enthusiasm."

"I thought your job description was whatever I needed?"

Her eyes narrowed dangerously, sharp eyeliner looking especially deadly. He'd probably pay for that remark in a strange, unexpected way later. She'd probably forget to order his favorite fancy gloves and make him use a brand he hated.

"Don't sass me."

Austin sighed. "I'm sorry, Nye. I just have a lot to think about."

Niyah mirrored his pose, leaning against the counter. "I'm probably going to regret this. Okay, spill."

Niyah usually didn't pay much attention to his personal affairs—his drama and hookups and angry girls who would show up at the shop. She'd cover for him, though, while he hid in the back office.

What was he supposed to tell her?

"Is it about that hot priest?"

Austin's face immediately flushed. Had they been so painfully obvious when Gideon had come to the shop?

Austin couldn't remember doing anything untoward, anything that would give bystanders a hint about the things Austin wanted to do to him.

"He ... he knew my brother."

Niyah's composure immediately softened, shoulders going loose and the corners of her eyes crinkling with sympathy.

Austin usually kept his history to himself; it wasn't something you would tell casual acquaintances.

Most people didn't know how to treat him after they knew. But he'd known Niyah for years. She was the office manager of a shop he worked for before he stole her when he left to open his own.

If memory served, he'd gotten fucking trashed on Luke's birthday one year and told her everything.

"I'm sorry, hun." She brushed a piece of hair off his forehead. It was a comforting platonic gesture, and he knew she wouldn't pry any deeper than that.

He was thankful that he knew Niyah wouldn't ask any more questions. Because he was so close. So close to confessing to someone, anyone, what he had done and how he felt.

Austin inhaled and exhaled, shaking out his shoulders like he was recentering himself. But Gideon had thrown his world completely off its axis, and a few breathing exercises were not going to fix that.

"Okay, booth layout. What you got?"

Kentucky weather in November could be fickle. Sometimes, it was cold; sometimes, it was still hot as balls.

On the day of the festival, the weather was perfect—chilly in the shade but warm when the sun peaked out from behind the clouds.

Their face painting booth turned out to be very popular with all manner of people. Austin had roped one of his other artists into showing up, and Niyah handled the money and the line.

Teenage girls came through in hordes for half-face butterfly wings and glittery unicorn horns.

A pretty girl with vibrant orange hair yapped his ear off while he painted her face, and her grumpy thick boyfriend glared at Austin's fingers on her chin the whole time. He could see bright neo-trad tattoos peeking out from under her loose sleeves.

Austin was a little surprised at the enthusiastic turnout. Family-friendly events weren't really his scene, but they had all kinds of vendors, food trucks, bounce houses, and even booze samples from a local winery.

Gideon should be happy with the results. The blonde soccer mom seemed pleased as she flitted around the parking lot, making sure everyone had what they needed.

Austin needed a wine sample. And to talk to Gideon, but the priest had been frustratingly hard to pin down. He was very popular, the star of the show.

Austin caught glimpses of his golden head through the crowd. He was wearing an expertly tailored pair of black slacks and a black shirt that nipped in his trim waist. He was back to being unattainable, in the uniform of his office, moving through the crowd like a shiny god.

Austin didn't like that. He liked Gideon naked, open, vulnerable, and honest, with the indentations of rope braids on his skin.

He noticed Gideon stopped to talk to most people, at most booth's, except for his.

What a coincidence.

Niyah breezed past Austin. She was wearing a burnt-orange jumpsuit and had let Austin paint pumpkins on her cheeks, their delicate, leafy vines curling up and around her brow bones.

"You're distracted," she said, refilling his rinse cup.

Austin huffed. "My hand hurts." He flexed the fingers on his dominant hand, feeling some of the joints pop. "These kids are vicious."

She smiled sweetly at him. "If you worked more than four hours a day, you'd have more stamina."

Austin barely resisted flicking paint at her. "Don't talk about my stamina."

She chortled to herself as she walked off to collect more money, and Austin chanced a glance around the crowd.

The golden head he'd been tracking all afternoon was gone. An irrational shred of fear stabbed him through the gut. It was irrational because nothing was wrong; nothing had happened to Gideon. He was probably behind a booth or went to get food. Or hell, went to piss.

They were in public.

But worse things had happened.

Austin's windpipe constricted uncomfortably. If he hadn't been tracking Gideon's precise location like a hawk, he probably wouldn't have even noticed his sudden absence.

But he had.

"Break," he barked at Niyah, leaving his stool and wiping paint-covered hands on his jeans.

"What? You can't leave!"

But he did.

Niyah would figure it out. He'd only be gone a few minutes. Just long enough to lay eyes on Gideon again.

He searched fruitlessly for a few minutes before his eyes caught on the ornate wooden door of St. Benedict's. It made the most sense.

The sanctuary was empty, dark, and quiet. Austin had to admit the church was a little creepy with no lights on and so many eyes watching—statues and stations. They could keep their judgements to themselves.

Austin pushed through a pair of unchurch-like metal doors that opened to the more civilian-friendly parts of the church.

It was still dark, the only illumination coming from motion-activated recessed lights in various corners.

He spied a door ajar, with a plaque that read *Parish Office* on the front.

Austin pushed the door open, and it fell open on silent hinges.

Gideon was there, his palms braced against the end of a desk, head bowed. He looked up and trapped Austin with that sharp blue gaze that was filled with so much unspoken emotion.

Relief hit Austin like a physical blow, sagging his shoulders. "You disappeared," he accused. He didn't just mean today.

Gideon inhaled, his elbows quivering; there was a light sheen of sweat across his forehead.

Austin softened, stepping into the office and pushing the door shut behind him. "Are you okay?"

Gideon looked about ready to spook, so Austin approached him slowly like he would a wild animal or nervous horse. Not that he had any experience with either.

Gideon tracked him with those eyes until they stood toe to toe.

Breath stuttered out of Gideon, his chest heaving.

Austin waited, the air filled with Gideon's labored breathing and a kind of tension he couldn't name. He waited until Gideon's body sagged, the old desk screeching as it took his weight.

"Can I touch you?" Austin asked.

Gideon nodded slowly, his eyes darting across Austin's face.

Austin laid his palm flat in the middle of Gideon's chest, his heartbeat a wild flicker.

Gideon wet his bottom lip, pulling at it nervously with his teeth. "Crowds get to me sometimes. It doesn't make much sense to me, the reason why. And just sometimes, not every time. I can go out in public without having a breakdown. I'm not—" He cut himself off abruptly, eyes flicking away.

What was he about to call himself? Broken? Defective?

Austin rubbed Gideon's chest, pressing down hard with his palm, feeling Gideon's racing heart slowly return to a more normal pace. "Whatever you think about yourself, it's not true. We deal with this shit the best we can. We cope with whatever we have."

Gideon brought a hand up and covered Austin's. His were bigger. He curled his fingers under Austin's slightly clammy palm.

Austin leaned forward and pressed a kiss to the back of Gideon's hand. "I've missed you." His lips brushed across Gideon's unmarked golden skin.

Gideon inhaled a ragged breath, their entwined fingers shuddering with it. "I've missed you too. But I can't miss you, Austin. I shouldn't. Yet I do. I swear to God, I do. But I can't have you."

Austin cupped Gideon's jaw, titling their mouths closer together but not closing the gap. His own heart pounded furiously. "Why not?"

A quiet, humorless laugh. "You know why."

A couple more centimeters, and Austin could feel Gideon's lips with every breath. "I know I have no right to ask this of you, and I know it makes me a selfish prick, but I want you to choose me."

# CHAPTER NINE
## GIDEON

*"I know I have no right to ask this of you, and I know it makes me a selfish prick, but I want you to choose me."*

Once again, Austin rearranged Gideon's entire world and dangled something in front of him he'd never thought he'd get to have.

A decision he never fathomed he'd have to make.

Austin's lips moved against his—a soft, sweet, forbidden temptation.

"I want you in my bed," he said. "I want you underneath me. I want you tied up over and over and over again."

Desire flamed hot, almost unbearably hot, in Gideon's pelvis. But Austin wasn't done tempting him with everything he couldn't have.

"I want to go on a date with you. I want to hold your hand in public. I want everyone to know you're mine."

The hand that had been tangled on Gideon's chest had drifted lower, playing with the buckle of his belt.

"You've been on your knees for me." Austin's voice was impossibly husky—velvet silk—against Gideon's mouth. "Now, I want to get on my knees for you." He cupped Gideon's erection. "Tell me you don't want the same things, and I'll go."

Gideon was many things. A sinner. Maybe a hypocrite. A confessor. A holder of people's darkest secrets, their shame. A sanctuary. A haven for lost souls. A shepherd.

But he was not a liar.

He crushed his mouth to Austin's, both hands grabbing his hips and mashing their pelvises together. Austin let out a small grunt of surprise, but then he was consuming Gideon's mouth with the same fervor, their tongues licking and lashing.

He could feel Austin's erection through his tight jeans, their cocks sliding and slotting against each other in such a perfect way it stole Gideon's breath. His rational thought.

Austin broke their kiss much too soon. "Let me, baby."

"Yes," Gideon said. He knew he was saying yes to this moment, but he also wanted to say yes to everything Austin was offering.

Austin smiled, nipped his lip, and went to his knees. He nuzzled at Gideon's groin, rubbing him through his slacks, and it was almost too much. He was so hard it hurt. If Austin kept going, he might come in his pants.

Austin barely undid Gideon's slacks, just opening them enough to pull down Gideon's briefs and draw out his throbbing dick.

He made a pleased noise in the back of his throat, his delicate thin fingers closing around the swollen red flesh. Austin had pretty, delicate hands, Gideon finally noticed.

"Such a big fat cock, baby. Do you wanna fuck my throat with it?"

Gideon moaned, sagging against the desk and falling back on his palms because he couldn't hold his body up a second longer.

Austin's mischievous eyes glowed in the dim light coming from the only window.

Thankfully, he did not require a verbal response, because Gideon was incapable of forming words. The only sounds leaving his mouth were grunts and whines as Austin closed his mouth over the tip.

He sucked at the delicate skin, tongue pressing into the slit. He licked all the precum away before making his way down Gideon's shaft and back up again.

A huff sounded. "You're not gonna fit."

Austin made a tight ring with his fingers, around the base of Gideon's cock, before stuffing him in his mouth as far down as he would go.

Gideon watched as Austin bobbed, his dick disappearing into the hot wetness of his throat. Austin hollowed his cheeks, the fingers around his base squeezing deliciously hard. Tears welled at the corners of his eyes. Gideon's hips bucked, and Austin choked but did not let go or stop or lose his rhythm.

He gazed up at Gideon with wet eyes, pink lips spread obscenely wide around his cock. Gideon throbbed, heat shooting up his spine, and then he was spurting down Austin's throat. He swallowed like it was nothing, licked Gideon clean, and then tucked him neatly back into his pants, smoothing the pleats down his thighs.

Gideon was shaking again, heart racing and throat dry for altogether different reasons than when he first sought refuge in his office.

Now, he wouldn't be able to sit in this office without remembering what had just happened. He'd probably get hard thinking about it, like he did almost every time he passed the altar where they'd kissed for the first time. The holy and the carnal inextricably linked in his head and his body.

Austin played with the curls over Gideon's ear, the soft brush of his fingertips sending shivers down his spine.

Gideon snagged his hips and drew Austin to him again. He didn't know what to do or what to say, so he kissed the tang of himself off Austin's lips.

"There is something I wanted to show you," Gideon said.

"Oh, a surprise? I love surprises." Austin's lean arms wrapped languidly around Gideon's body.

He wasn't ready for those arms to fall away yet, so he searched the top of the desk for one piece of elusive paper. It took longer than anticipated, and Austin laughed.

"I wanted it to be a surprise, but I also don't want to do it if you think it's inappropriate." He held up the paper.

"Lover, I live for inappropriateness."

Gideon flushed as Austin's eyes fell to the paper. He read it once, paused, and then took the sheet from Gideon to read it again.

Gideon suddenly felt horribly self-conscious. "You have the final say. I'll rip it up and forget it was ever a thought if you don't think it's okay."

"The Luke Davenport Memorial Scholarship." Austin blinked, his thick lashes fluttering. "Gideon, what is this?"

Gideon's pulse thrummed so hard in his head it was hard to hear himself speaking. "It's a letter proposing the scholarship to the principal and school board of our high school. Paige has been helping me with the logistics. It'll be for kids who want to play competitive ball but can't afford the expenses. You remember how much our moms would complain about new bats? I've been wanting to do something like this for a while now, but I didn't want to do it without you, or at least without you knowing about it, and I've been such a fucking"—Gideon took a deep breath, finally—"coward."

Austin had been right about him. Gideon had been running. He had run from his past, his trauma. He had buried himself in community projects and acts of service, anything to assuage the guilt. He had buried himself in theology, in obscure psychological theories, all in an effort to understand the impossible.

Gideon licked his suddenly dry lips. "Then I saw you in the Creek, and it almost felt like … fate."

Call it fate or destiny, or providence or an act of God, but their paths had crossed again for a reason.

Austin chuckled. "You think we're fated, huh?"

Gideon flushed. "Not exactly what I said."

Austin let the proposal flutter back down on top of the desk, his hand coming to rest in the curve of Gideon's back. "It's perfect," he said. "I like it more than the bench they did for the ten-year anniversary." His fingers stroked down the vertebrae at the base of Gideon's spine. "I have to go back to working *your* festival before Niyah realizes how long I've been gone. Think about what I said, before."

*"I know I have no right to ask this of you, and I know it makes me a selfish prick, but I want you to choose me."*

Gideon suppressed a sigh. "It may not be that simple, Austin." His voice didn't come out sounding like his own. He sounded like a man resigned to a fate he didn't want anymore.

Austin cupped his face. "Think about it. Don't give me an answer now. Come find me when you're done with the self-flagellation, and let me do it instead. But, like, in a fun way."

Gideon's brows rose.

"What? I googled it." He pecked Gideon's lips quickly and then was gone.

Gideon was left alone in his dark, empty office, staring at the crucifix on the wall.

# CHAPTER TEN
## GIDEON

Gideon didn't have an answer for Austin the next day.

He didn't have an answer a week later.

People quit jobs all the time for all sorts of reasons. But Gideon's job was supposed to be something more than just a job. It was supposed to be a calling, a vocation. He wasn't supposed to be able to walk away on a whim.

But Austin didn't feel like a whim.

He felt preordained. Inevitable.

So, Gideon emailed his scholarship proposal to the current principal of their old high school. She thought it was a wonderful idea and wanted to speak with him in person.

So, Gideon drove the four hours to the high school to meet her, have her fawn over his generosity of spirit, and hand over his check. It was a nice, healthy start to the fund.

Five years of scrimping and saving, of skipping a meal or being late on a bill, as long as he could put his fifty dollars in the savings account. He realized this also may have been another form of penance. Self-flagellation, as Austin had so elegantly put it.

Austin had also grossly underrepresented the ten-year memorial. It was more than just a bench. It was a whole damn garden on the front lawn, sprung up around a rustic, redwood gazebo—which was not just a bench. The garden was neat and clearly maintained.

There was a brass plaque at the entrance to the gazebo, nestled between roses and lilacs. Eight names were embossed on the surface—five students and three teachers.

He didn't read the names. He didn't need to. They were seared on his soul.

Gideon rubbed his palms on his jeans as he ascended the little steps and took a seat on the bench that ran the perimeter. He was in mostly civilian clothes: jeans, a black button-down, and a black cardigan, minus his clerical collar. He didn't feel comfortable wearing it while he was in such a state of doubt.

It was warm, sunlight speckling the treated wood as it slatted in through the decorative lattice.

Gideon cleared his throat, folding his hands together in his lap—an imitation of hands folded together in prayer.

He didn't know why he was nervous. He did this all the time—talking, praying, to a god he wasn't even sure existed. His faith hadn't taken him that far.

He wasn't brave enough to go to the cemetery, so this sunny, quiet place would have to do.

"Well, I fucked your brother," he said. And then he laughed to himself, to the air. His throat felt thick and heavy, as if filled with cotton, even though he had just finished talking to the principal.

He cleared his throat, shifting a bit on the bench seat. "You'd be proud of him, I think. He's grown up, mostly." Gideon shook his head, thinking of Austin's floppy hair and his devil-may-care attitude. "He owns his own business. Can you believe that? Maybe it's not so surprising. He always was the smart one. Quiet, bookish. Always had ink on his fingers."

That little habit had driven their mom mad. Austin was always leaving little smudges on the furniture, the walls, and his clothes.

Gideon sighed, tipping his head up into a shaft of sunlight. What was he supposed to do? What choice was he supposed to make? His heart or his guilt?

A breeze brushed across his face, and Gideon could feel the coolness of tears drying on his cheeks. He hadn't even realized they'd slipped free.

"I'm so sorry, Luke. I'm sorry, my friend."

Then he closed his eyes, clasped his hands, bowed his head, and finally prayed.

# CHAPTER ELEVEN

## AUSTIN

Austin hadn't expected Gideon's choice to be easy, but he had also not expected it to take so fucking long.

Two weeks.

He hadn't heard from him yet. Again.

It was unusual for Austin to lay all his cards on the table, and the unknowable, squirmy feeling in his gut was why. He was usually the one doing the rejecting, not the one being rejected.

His phone vibrated on the island.

The screen flashed: *Mom*.

Austin hesitated for a heartbeat. His relationship with his mother had not been the same since Luke died. She had retreated into her grief, somehow forgetting that she still had a living son who needed her.

But he could never blame her for that.

He answered. "Momma."

There was a beat of silence on the other end. "Your old school called me. Someone set up a scholarship fund in Luke's name."

"Oh, yeah." He traced the dark veins of the marble.

"Did you know? Who? The local paper called too. They want to do some kind of human-interest piece." She sighed, and there was the clink of a glass in the background.

"Uh, yeah. It was Gideon. Gray," he added, in case she had forgotten the name of the boy who had practically lived with them for years, he and Luke stuck together like two halves of the same whole.

"Ah, yes, Gideon. How ..." She cleared her throat. "How is he? Have you heard from him?"

The back of Austin's neck heated. "Yeah, Mom, we've ... reconnected. He lives here. In Cedar Creek."

There was a knock at the door.

"I've got to go. I'll talk to you later."

"Okay, baby. We should talk more. You'll come home soon, right?" His mother couldn't bear the thought of leaving the place where Luke died; Austin couldn't get away fast enough.

Austin sucked on his teeth. "Yes, Mom."

The call disconnected.

His pizza was early, but when Austin opened the door, it wasn't a delivery man darkening his doorstep.

Austin's breath hitched.

Gideon was there, one hand braced on the door frame, hair mussed and his cheeks red.

"Did you run here?"

Gideon's breath sawed out of him. "No, I walked up the stairs. And then back down. And then back up."

Austin's heart hammered his ribs. Was that good or bad?

He stepped back to give Gideon enough room to enter the apartment. "You better come in after all that."

Gideon hesitated, his fingers flexing against the dark wood. Austin noted that he was missing his customary black, wearing instead a pair of jeans and gray sweater. That had to be a good sign, right?

"I've requested to be released from the clerical state." His voice was ragged and husky, but his eyes were bright as they bore into Austin's. Those blue orbs flicked to his mouth.

The invisible weight that had been crushing Austin's chest for weeks lightened. "You chose me?"

Gideon stepped closer, and Austin's pulse pounded in his wrists and ears.

Gideon's hand landed on the back of his neck like a fiery brand. "I chose you."

Then his mouth was there, his forehead pressed to Austin's, his lips warm and urgent. Austin collapsed against his body, and then they were nothing but hands and grunts and harsh breathing.

Someone kicked the door closed, and then clothes were being shucked. Gideon tugged on Austin's hair, kissed his jaw, and nipped on his earlobe and the delicate skin of his throat.

It only took a few panting moments before Austin had Gideon spread out on his bed, his arms bound above his head.

It was a simple bind, something Austin could almost do with his eyes closed. The rope wrapped around Gideon's wrists and down his arms to his biceps. Gideon's hands were clasped together, his fingers twitching.

Austin knelt between his spread thighs, one hand on Gideon's heaving stomach muscles and the other on the thick muscle of his leg. He loved the way Gideon twitched under his touch, the way his lips parted, and the way he gave himself up so easily.

Austin ran his hand up Gideon's thigh, over the soft crux between his thigh and hip, until he circled the base of his dick.

Gideon groaned, back arching. Austin stroked, feeling Gideon grow thicker under his palm.

"Do you think you'll regret it one day?"

Gideon blinked, dark lashes sweeping his cheeks. "What?"

Austin figured it probably wasn't fair to ask that of Gideon at this *precise* moment, when he was so literally in the palm of his hand.

Gideon's dick jerked, and his teeth sunk into his bottom lip.

Why was that so fucking hot? Austin pressed his hips to Gideon's, their cocks sliding together. Austin had never claimed to play fair. In fact, he'd already warned Gideon he was selfish.

Gideon's hips rose to meet Austin's lazy thrusts. "No." He gasped. "I don't think I will. It was about punishment, not about faith. And I—" He groaned as Austin squeezed him. "I'm tired of living like that."

Austin grinned down at him. "You thought I'd be a better punishment?"

Gideon's lips twitched. He was gazing up at Austin with an odd expression, his eyes and mouth soft, that pretty red flush covering his cheeks. Austin was hesitant to name that look, but it made his pulse race so fast it felt like he couldn't breathe.

"You're not a punishment. You're ... something new. Something hopeful."

Austin leaned down and captured Gideon's mouth. The kiss was slow and sweet, in contrast with Gideon's bound hands and Austin's hard grip on his cock. He kissed the man until he was breathless and leaking over his hand.

"That's good enough, for now," Austin whispered.

"What else could you possibly want?" Gideon's words scraped against Austin's throat.

"Everything, Gideon Gray. I want everything."

# EPILOGUE

Gideon had a first date.

The butterflies rioting in his stomach were more appropriate for a boy, and not a thirty-two-year-old man, but there was nothing to be done about them. Gideon had never been on a date before. He didn't date in high school, or college.

A *first*, first date.

He'd agonized over his outfit choice, like that would make or break Austin's opinion of him, before settling on a hunter green cable-knit sweater and a pair of dark wash jeans. Then, he agonized over his cologne choice.

It was an odd, unsettling feeling to worry about his appearance. Before, he just worried about being clean and presentable. He wasn't concerned about his looks. He was unnotable in his black. Now, he wasn't.

The bishop had called to voice his concerns, but Gideon had told him the truth. Mostly. Omitting only the sordid details.

He doubted his faith.

He couldn't lead his flock anymore.

His heart was someplace else.

After that, leaving the Church had been simpler than expected. There had been other logistics to work out. He needed a new place to live, a new job. He could do anything, be anyone, and the options made him dizzy.

He was still working on the job, but the housing situation resolved itself easily enough.

Mrs. Della had a small apartment over her garage that used to be for her kids, but they had all moved out of town and she was willing to offer it for rent. Only to Gideon, because she knew he was a nice boy with strong arms for yardwork (her words). If Della was curious about Gideon's sudden return to role of layperson, she had yet to pry.

Her timing was impeccable, and once again, Gideon had the feeling it was fated. He was finally in the right place, at the right time. He was on the right path. He was making a fresh start. He could make different choices, live a little for himself and not to assuage his guilt. His survivor's guilt, as Austin had so succinctly put it.

He had also begun researching trauma therapists, but that was a bridge he was still working up to crossing.

Two short honks sounded from the street.

His ride was here.

Austin drove a tiny, compact car that was almost too small for the both of them. Gideon felt his hair brushing the roof.

They were quiet during the drive. Austin hadn't told him where they were going, but Gideon recognized the area of town they were in.

He chuckled. "The zoo, Austin? Really?"

Austin grinned as he parked. "I like the zoo."

It was a beautiful, chilly, fall day and they almost had the zoo to themselves, since school was still in session and it was a weekday.

They meandered through the park; Austin had a sketchbook tucked under one arm and about a half-dozen pencils and charcoals in his shirt pocket.

"Ooh, the HerpAquarium!" Austin grabbed Gideon's hand and dragged him into the cool quiet of the HerpAquarium exhibit. Based on the copious amounts of snakes, bugs, and moths inked into his skin, Gideon wasn't surprised.

They walked through the exhibit, passing tanks filled with all kinds of creepy crawlies Gideon couldn't name. Austin could, though, and had a fact ready for almost each one.

"Did you know vampire bats can consume sixty percent of their own weight during feeding?"

"No, I did not." Gideon's voice was warm with laughter. Then his face heated as he realized Austin had never dropped his hand. Their fingers were twined together, a braid of ownership, of acknowledgement. A public claiming, something Gideon assumed he had forsaken years ago.

He gently squeezed Austin's fingers and Austin squeezed back.

They meandered until Austin decided he'd found a good place to stop and Gideon wasn't sure what parameters were used in the judgement.

It was a quiet spot, dim and cool, with backless benches running between the creature tanks.

Austin sat, propping an ankle over one of his knees and then settling his sketchbook on his lap.

Gideon straddled the bench, his thighs spreading around Austin's body.

"I thought this was a date," he said.

Austin thumbed through the pages. "It is."

"Then why does it look like you're working?"

"This is for fun."

Austin flashed a grin that sent warmth sparking through Gideon's chest. If he had any lingering doubts, that smile, the lightness in Austin's eyes, the sweet dip of his upper lip, chased them all away.

Gideon snatched Austin's wrist to stop his flipping. One of the pages had caught his eye. It was a mess of random doodles, pencil smears, and maybe food, but there was a familiar face in the middle.

It was Gideon's face. Curls, serious eyes, the glass of bourbon by his parted mouth.

Gideon frowned. "Do I really look like that?"

The portrait was quick, just a sketch, but somehow Austin had managed to capture the tortured downturn of Gideon's mouth.

Austin cocked his head, making a big show of examining the drawing. "No, not anymore. You've unfortunately lost some of that mid-2000s angsty emo flair."

Gideon fisted Austin's hair and yanked his head back, baring the pillar of his throat. Austin's eyes flashed with heat and challenge.

"I never had an emo phase."

"Could've fooled me," Austin rasped. His throat bobbed with a swallow.

They were alone—for now—but who knew how long that might last. The smooth skin of Austin's jaw, his throat, were begging for attention.

Previously, Gideon would have never dared to be so brazen. He had denied himself for so long. There were no rules now, no barriers. Austin had claimed him earlier by taking his hand and Gideon longed to do the same.

His body trembled and burned. He leaned forward and kissed the delicate skin under Austin's jaw. He could feel Austin smile under his lips.

Just one, chaste, saccharine kiss because they were still in public after all.

Gideon pulled back and mussed Austin's carefully coiffed hair before letting him go.

"You look happier now." Austin turned to a blank page in his sketchbook. "Like you're finally not carrying the whole damn world on your shoulders."

Happy.

Was Gideon happy? Was that what he could call the bright, warm tightness in his chest? Gideon had almost forgotten what happiness felt like. Every time he felt that spark, he would stamp it out because he didn't deserve to be happy. He deserved his punishment. Because Luke was dead. And Luke was not happy.

But was Gideon's misery truly what his best friend would have wanted?

Gideon inhaled and exhaled slowly, trying to relieve some of the pressure. He knew the road would be long. His habits and thought patterns and opinion of himself would be hard to break. But it was a start. A new start.

Austin glanced up. "Are you okay, babe?"

That warm little light flared again. Gideon smiled and scooted closer so that his knee could touch Austin's thigh.

"Yeah, I'm happy. You make me happy."

Austin booped him on the nose with the end of his pencil, one eyebrow raised. "Is that all?"

No, it wasn't all. There was so much still to say, to do, to discover. But Gideon's freedom was still new, his heart still raw.

"For now," he said.

# Afterword

Thank you for reading *Rope Break*!
I hope you enjoyed Gideon and Austin's story and are
ready to prop up your feet and stay for a long time in Cedar
Creek, Kentucky. A good time is guaranteed!
Reviews are one of the best ways to support an author, so
I would love you forever if you left one (or even just some
stars!) somewhere on the internet (also, tell you friends
about the BPC!).
Be sure you're following me for updates about the series.
Who's next? You'll just have to wait and see!

Did you really, *really* enjoy this story and want to dive
deeper into the Jessica-verse?
I would be absolutely tickled if you joined me on Patreon! You can get free eBooks, sticker mailings, be-

hind-the-scenes updates, bonus content, early access, and can start reading my unhinged paranormal romance serial, *Guilty As Sin*.

# About the Author

**J.L. Minyard** is the not-so-secret pen name of award-winning young adult author Jessica Minyard. Jessica is an author, poet, ISTJ, Sagittarius, and boy mom who lives and writes from the bluegrass.

Check out both her contemporary series:

Penn Warren University

Bluegrass Performance Center

For freebies, sneak peeks, and other updates, head to jessicaminyard.com to sign up for her newsletter or join her on Patreon.

Follow her on social media:

facebook.com/jessicaminyardbooks

instagram.com/callmeshashka

tiktok.com/@jessicawritesromance

amazon.com/stores/J.L.-Minyard/author/B0B7R171CP

# MINYARD'S MINIONS

# SEE THE KINKTOBER SERIES

Be sure to check out the other stories in the K!nktober series! Thirty-four authors came together to bring you wild and fantastical tales in every kind of genre and with amazing imagination. From ghosts and robots, to angels and pirates, there's something here for everyone.

HITCHHIKER X PRIMAL PLAY

*Haze of Sin*

Sloane Sabel

Smoke was on a mission when the golden eyes of a hitchhiker caught their gaze. Kae stood at the edge of the battered road, lips chapped and skin bruised. Smoke thought Kae might make a tasty snack—until a seductive rendezvous in the woods turns into a wild fight for survival.

Amazon: https://books2read.com/hazeofsinknktober

Goodreads: https://www.goodreads.com/book/show/229259703-haze-of-sin

FAE X CUMFLATION

### *Convincing His Little Bee*

Sage L Mattison

Winning the fae in the auction was the only way to keep him safe, but Tor knew he had to work hard to convince his fated that he wasn't like other creatures who had bid on him. An MX Romance between a swear-happy bossy bottom fae, and a kind-hearted drakonid who's ready and willing to be bossed around.

Amazon: https://amzn.to/3FGBIck

Goodreads: https://www.goodreads.com/book/show/235778932-convincing-his-little-bee

GARGOYLE X PIERCINGS

### *Carved in Desire*

Cheyenne Browning

I get the surprise of a lifetime when my new house I've just moved into has this gorgeous statue that is apparently a real life gargoyle. Passions burn as I find out the truth and see where the desire takes me. Pierced with desire and fully satiated with the woman worthy of my love.

Amazon: https://books2read.com/carvedindesireknktober

Goodreads: https://www.goodreads.com/book/show/235643104-carved-in-desire

PRIEST X SHIBARI

### *Rope Break*

J. L. Minyard

Father Gideon Gray has spent most of his life haunted by guilt and ghosts. But the one man he should never want, his best friend's younger brother, doesn't want his penance. He wants Gideon's submission.

Amazon: https://books2read.com/ropebreak

Goodreads: https://www.goodreads.com/book/show/228981154-rope-break

ARACHNID X SUSPENSION

### The Web of Athena

M.L. Eaden

When this unassuming accountant discovers The Playground, a premier sex club on The Firebaugh Resort, she books herself for a free consultation. With Mx. Beverly, an eccentric performer, and their group of nymphs, Melody re-discovers herself in ways she only dreamed about.

Amazon: https://www.amazon.com/dp/B0F8YRWPHH

Goodreads: https://www.goodreads.com/book/show/234295582-the-web-of-athena

NAGA X ANAL

### Falling for the Serpent God

Daffodil Rae

One day on an outing with her friends, Aria saves an injured serpent. Thanat, a divine naga falls for Aria's nurturing spirit after spending a week in her care disguised as a normal serpent. After sparks fly between them, Thanat desires to grant Aria's most sacred wish, for his own satisfaction.

Amazon: https://books2read.com/fallingfortheserpentgod

Goodreads: https://www.goodreads.com/book/show/234982670-falling-for-the-serpent-god

Slasher x Kidnapping

**Slasher**

Roslyn St. Clair

He's a dark, deranged, djinn-ridden hero with a need for revenge and a penchant for slashing, murder, kidnapping, stalking ... and now, Lila. She may be on his k*ll list, but sometimes a man just has to go off book when he loses his heart. DARK, spicy romance.

Amazon: https://books2read.com/slasherknktober

Goodreads: https://www.goodreads.com/book/show/228992723-slasher

Yeti x Sensory Deprivation

**Chosen by the Yeti**

Cassandra Elizzabeth

Isen steps into the sacred cave as a willing sacrifice, desire burning brighter than fear. Will the Spirit of the Mountain choose her as his own or will she be forced to return to the village, marked forever as unwanted?

Amazon: https://books2read.com/u/3RM0DL

Goodreads: https://www.goodreads.com/book/show/238608392-chosen-by-the-yeti

Angel x Crossdressing

### The Kiss Before the Fall

Ravi Novais

She is fallen, feared, unrepentant, and the one temptation he cannot resist. Their hunger is forbidden, their obsession is mutual. And in a world where gods drink secrets and monsters feed on desire, worship may cost him more than his wings.

Amazon: https://books2read.com/thekissbeforethefall

Goodreads: https://www.goodreads.com/book/show/236450931-the-kiss-before-the-fall

Vampire x Triple Penetration

### Dark, Stormy Night

VL Banx

Dmitri wants his vampire queen to be satisfied in every way possible, so he and Natasia host a debaucherously dangerous dinner party to find the perfect sacrifices for their pleasure.

Amazon: https://a.co/d/bjXtiHK

Goodreads: https://www.goodreads.com/book/show/239454997

Military x Wax Play

### The Trouble with Sprites

Elliot Ason

Luther has returned home, battle weary and hoping for a good time. His interest piques when Olympia, a raven-haired little fire sprite, catches his eye. He'll see to it that he has her for the evening. All of her.

Amazon: https://books2read.com/u/bpPyO9

Goodreads: https://www.goodreads.com/book/show /231361331-the-trouble-with-sprites

Doctor x Somnophilia

### *Side Effects*

Frederick A. Zaberisk

Dr. Matthias Fournier is a no-nonsense man, and the idea of sex is a far off concept. That is, until his colleague, Luka Blanchett — a constant thorn in his side — has an "idea". Will this be a one-off fling, or will it become something more?

Amazon: https://www.amazon.com/dp/B0F3QKYM HX

Goodreads: https://www.goodreads.com/book/show /231018424-side-effects

Leprechaun x Hucow

### *Leprechaun's Lucky Hucow*

Marilyn Barr

When an ambitious hucow and an innovative leprechaun build a milk distribution business that's the envy of all Magmell, will mixing business with pleasure be their downfall, or what allows them to survive the unthinkable? The beasts usually capture them, but will they have the courage to fight for what they've built after they've captured each other's hearts?

Amazon: https://a.co/d/iVCyvcB

Goodreads: https://www.goodreads.com/book/show
/231204049-leprechaun-s-lucky-hucow

ALIEN X EXHIBITIONISM

***Let Them Watch***

E.V. Sauvage

After catching her boyfriend making a sex tape with her best friend, Lynna ends up with a non-refundable ticket to *be* the show at the Interspace Cabaret, the notorious exhibitionist club on Cestàhar, and is too stubborn to call it a loss.

So, now, she has only weeks to find someone willing to have sex on stage, and she doesn't even care if he's human.

Amazon: https://books2read.com/u/bxp8LD

Goodreads: https://www.goodreads.com/book/show
/239189293-let-them-watch

WRANGLER X BRANDING

***Ride a Wrangler***

Jorjor Battle

A Ranch Princess finds out what it is meant to be owned by a Wrangler.

Amazon: https://books2read.com/rideawrangler

Goodreads: https://www.goodreads.com/book/show
/231394875-ride-a-wrangler

SUPERHERO/VILLAIN X TEACHER/STUDENT

***Reestablishing Shot***

aurora light

A superhero in film school falls into a BDSM relationship with her screenwriting teacher. It's her first healthy relationship, but her friends disagree—and the secret her teacher is hiding could prove them right.

Amazon: https://books2read.com/b/reestablishing-shot

Goodreads: https://www.goodreads.com/book/show/239641170-reestablishing-shot

### Wizard x Breath Play

#### *Elements of Choking*

Sofia Graves

The darkest wizard in the realm needs a conduit ... and her kink is the perfect trigger.

Amazon: https://books2read.com/elementsofchoking

Goodreads: https://www.goodreads.com/book/show/236785476-elements-of-choking

### Werewolf x Electric Play

#### *Shock and Paws*

Latrexa Nova

What's a werewolf to do with a human taser for a boyfriend—let him help with my revenge ... or use his powers for more pleasurable things?

If Mathieu was my tormentor, I would have begged for more.

So now my teeth ache for two things: Revenge ... and Mathieu.

Amazon: https://books2read.com/shockandpaws

Goodreads: https://www.goodreads.com/book/show /235852199-shock-paws

SIREN X BREEDING

*His Siren Prince*

Abigail Hunter

When Commander Carrion returns from the war with the Demon King's head, he is offered a prize, and there's only one thing he desires. But the Prince Azul wants more than one night together, and Carrion becomes obsessed with breeding his siren prince until he is stuffed full and his seed is planted.

Amazon: https://books2read.com/hissirenprince

Goodreads: https://www.goodreads.com/book/show /228553716-his-siren-prince

CYCLOPS X OFFICE SEX

*The Flower and the Titan*

Gracie Cooper

Flor Domingo moved away from the hustle and bustle of the city and into the cozy world of small-town living. Things were looking up when she was offered the job at The Bookstore.

The job: get the place up and running by the end of the week. Oh, and don't fall in love with your cyclops boss. Easy peasy.

Amazon: https://books2read.com/theflowerandtheti tan

Goodreads: https://www.goodreads.com/book/show
/234586277-the-flower-and-the-titan

Orc x Temperature Play

### Just A Small Town Orc

Bevin Shea

Thrakh, Maplewicket's own golden citizen and respect-
ed baseball coach, is thrown into chaos when he recognizes
a player's curvy-as-sin aunt as his fated mate. Stevie doesn't
know what to make of the incredibly handsome, yet equal-
ly confusing orc who insulted her before asking her out on
a date. With the help of the town during their renowned
Halloween festivities, Thrakh pulls out all the stops to woo
Stevie, but can he convince his mate that just a small town
orc can love and care for her like she deserves?

Amazon: books2read.com/justasmalltownorc

Goodreads: https://www.goodreads.com/book/show
/234557504-just-a-small-town-orc

Demon x Fisting

### The Demon's Vow

L.S. Monroe

A night of Halloween fun turns dark when an insatiable, seductive demon is summoned, and poor, unsus-
pecting Lukas finds himself chosen as its eternal mate.

Amazon: https://books2read.com/thedemonsvow

Goodreads: https://www.goodreads.com/book/show
/238446006-the-demon-s-vow

Biker x Orgy

### Headless Not Heartless

A.A. Fairview

A widow is visited by her deceased wife, but death changes everything.

Amazon: https://a.co/d/6pMKAK8

Goodreads: https://www.goodreads.com/book/show /238641394-headless-not-heartless

MERPERSON X BUKAKE

### Taste of the Briny Deep

Coral Alejandra Moore

A submissive witch meets a dangerous merman whose appetites tempt her to give in to the dark desires she's been craving.

Amazon: https://www.amazon.com/dp/B0F5W8N6 MG

Goodreads: https://www.goodreads.com/book/show /232023383-taste-of-the-briny-deep

ELF X FLOGGING/WHIPPING

### On His Knees

Pix Pentham

In a world where magic is highly-regulated, a trouble-making elf gets tangled up with a workaholic cop - and quickly discovers there may be a desire to bend the knee beneath the surface of that stone-grey skin.

Amazon: https://a.co/d/fWRdHCm

Goodreads: https://www.goodreads.com/book/show
/239005721-on-his-knees

SATYR X PEGGING

### *Sating the Satyr*

Biblio Barbie

Professor Fylis Thistlehorn, a satyr who has suppressed
his primal instincts to fit into academia, finds his life
turned upside down when his troll best friend introduces
him to Mistress Jade, a confident human dominatrix.
What begins as an uncomfortable experiment in submission gradually evolves into a deep, unexpected connection.

Amazon: https://amzn.to/42jtSxz

Goodreads: https://www.goodreads.com/book/show
/230508105-sating-the-satyr

SHADOW MONSTER X HEAT/KNOTTING

### *A Final Girl Halloween*

RE Johnson

Wreak some havoc this Halloween, and step back into
the world of Amelia and her Monster Man—plus the curious detective they picked up along the way.

Noah gets his own personal revenge, and Amelia learns
that one loose thread is still hanging, one she intends to
**cut**.

Amazon: https://books2read.com/u/bzNK2L

Goodreads: https://www.goodreads.com/book/show
/232566201-a-final-girl-halloween

MINOTAUR X VOYEURISM

### Fan Service

Robin Jo Margaret

As a famous adult entertainer, getting familiar with a fan is rarely a good idea, but Rory finds herself making an exception for Bryce, the polite and handsome minotaur who has been her supporter for a little over a year. Bryce, however, is not the only one interested in her.

Amazon: https://books2read.com/fanserviceknktober

Goodreads: https://www.goodreads.com/book/show /238522365-fan-service

### Ghost x Hole in the Wall

### Ghostly Shenanigans

Kat Holiday

As a previously housebound ghost, Astrid has no clue what to do with her (technical) new found freedom. Luckily she's got a group of housemates more than willing to get up to some (ghostly) shenanigans alongside her, and help her test out her new "abilities".

Amazon: https://books2read.com/ghostlyshenanigans

Goodreads: https://www.goodreads.com/book/show /234652359-ghostly-shenanigans

### God/Goddess x Mirrors

### Many Reflections of a Storm

Delilah Dare

Terra was used to feeling watched, but she always chalked it up to her exhibitionist kink. She'd never considered an air god with Wizard Daddy vibes and his werewolf boyfriend were observing her through the mirrors, biding their time to steal her away. When they do, she discovers a home she'd always longed for, and a dormant power the land hadn't seen in centuries.

Amazon: https://books2read.com/manyreflectionsof astorm

Goodreads: https://www.goodreads.com/book/show /238070106-many-reflections-of-a-storm

Pirate x Forced Genderswap

***Corsairs and Corsets***

Frederick A. Zaberisk

Lord Alistair Beaumont has an idea — to capture a ruthless pirate and "refine" him into something more... feminine. Said pirate, Finnegan, strongly resists this idea. Will Alistair prevail, or will Finnegan refuse to adapt?

Amazon: https://books2read.com/corsairsandcorsets

Goodreads: https://www.goodreads.com/book/show /238647706-corsairs-and-corsets